THE SUN WOLVES

A NOVELLA

DENVER C. BINION

COPYRIGHT

Copyright © 2024 Denver Binion

This is a work of fiction. Names, characters, places and incidents are fictitious. Any resemblance to actual persons, living or dead, events, or locales is coincidental. All rights reserved. This book may not be reproduced in whole or in part without the express written permission of the copyright holder.

DEDICATION

This book is for Ana, the love of my life.

I couldn't have done this without you.

Table of Contents

CHAPTER ONE 5

CHAPTER TWO 20

CHAPTER THREE 35

CHAPTER FOUR 51

CHAPTER FIVE 66

CHAPTER SIX 84

CHAPTER SEVEN 99

CHAPTER EIGHT 113

CHAPTER NINE 125

ABOUT THE AUTHOR 145

CHAPTER ONE

"Blasphemer!"
The cry struck Elya harder than any whip, burned hotter than any fire.
"You have blasphemed against the Order, blasphemed against Mighty Ballian, and are unworthy to be called his Daughter!" the old, raspy voice continued in a hiss, the woman who was speaking nearly bending over her walking stick as she shouted. Spittle, wet and hot, spattered her face at the woman's nearness, but she dare not move to wipe it away.
"Mother, I only-" she tried to say, to explain, but Mother Moira's open palm struck her cheek before another word could leave her lips, the crisp *crack* of it filling the chapel. Elya's face burned now for more than one reason. She could hear them all whispering behind her, the other Daughters. She knew what this meant.
Still, fate was not often something one could accept so easily.
"You will not speak another word! You will not dishonor our Lord Ballian with your serpent's tongue!"

Moira snapped, yet Elya knew there was no way she would leave it at that. Not when their very lives were at stake.

"Mother, the Horde is only a few days away! Everyone here is in danger! I only want-"

This time, when the blow came, she was prepared for it. It didn't sink her low, didn't rip away her dignity. She took it with a glare, with the grit she had spent her entire life trying to hide from the world. She spat this time, and hers was bloody, but Ballian's own crown it felt *good.*

Moira saw it, saw the defiance, and pulled back as if stung. Then, her lips twisting in some gross caricature of a smile, she stood to her full height and addressed the room.

"It brings me no joy to do this, Elya, but you have left me no choice. The tenets of the Order are very clear, straight from the Blessed Scriptures themselves. 'All homes of the Order are sacred and shall be treated as such. To abandon the home is to abandon oneself, and to turn thy face from Ballian's Love.' Yet this very day, you have not only suggested, but *argued unrepentantly* for abandoning this holy abbey!" the Mother declared.

This, Elya knew, was not for her benefit. The theatrics, the show of false remorse, it was for the others behind her. The rest of the Daughters. She was using Elya as an example, and in so doing was condemning them all to die.

It made her sick.

"Don't do this, Mother. Please. You're all going to die," Elya begged quietly, her voice barely above a whisper, loud enough only for the head of the abbey to hear. The older woman looked down her nose with a sneer.

"You doubt even our Lord's ability to protect us from harm. Has your faith always been such a sad, weak thing?" Moira shook her head, then turned back to the podium behind her, upon which lay the abbey's copy of the Scriptures. Reaching one ancient, wrinkled hand to its cracked leather cover, she said the words that would forever end the life Elya knew.

"From this moment forward you, Elya, Daughter of No One, are excommunicated from the Order. You may never again set foot within the walls of this abbey, or any other holy ground claimed by our Lord Ballian. Furthermore, none of our Order shall ever speak with you again; your words are a poison, and we shall not partake. Begone from this place, and never return."

They were like a physical blow, but once more she refused to show her pain.

Elya stood, slowly, until she was fully on her feet. She looked down at Mother Moira, her height of nearly five feet and ten inches more than enough for her to look down on the other women of Talwich Abbey. Now she used it as a shield, breathing deep and releasing all of the expectations and unhealthy beliefs that had been instilled in her for her entire life through the simple act of a step toward Moira. A single movement, her lips peeled back in a wide smile. The satisfaction she felt when the old crone flinched almost made it all worth it. Almost.

She would never hurt her. Elya knew that. Moira did too. None of the other Daughters had even seen it happen. But the two of them would always know that in the end, the Mother of Talwich Abbey was afraid of *her*, not the other way around.

Elya turned and strode down the center aisle of the ancient chapel, its painted stone and cracked mosaic ceiling a thing of her past. She looked around, though, searching the faces of many of the other Daughters. Almost all of them averted their eyes, afraid to meet hers and draw the ire of Moira, and that was the real blow of her excommunication. These young women, some of them yet girls, were the only family she knew. Her sisters, each and every one. Yet now that family was taken from her, and none of them would say a thing to help.

"You're all going to pretend you can't hear me, and that's fine... but please, save yourselves while you can. Your lives are more important than any place," she said aloud, sadly, into the dead silence. Then she lifted her shoulders, turned and left.

The dulled clicking of her shoes on the stone hall faded into the back of her mind more and more with every room she passed, each of them sending memories flooding through her brain. The first time she and Penna were assigned washing duty. Hours spent with her closest friends up past curfew, discussing the Scriptures and Mother Moira and the abbey... anything and everything that made up their small lives. Even the endless days of bland food in the mess hall, warmed by the sisterhood that made life at Talwich Abbey bearable.

Twenty-four years, she lived here.

It was all she knew, all that she could remember. She was left with the Order of Bellian as a baby, abandoned for who knows what reason by parents who she did not know. There were fates that could have been much worse, but now it did not matter

Her memories and introspection came to a halt as she reached the dormitories and stepped into her closet of a room. There was not much there. A tiny bed, a couple sets of the same tan robes that were the only clothing she had ever owned, a simple bag with a sling and a small leather water bladder, a pair of work boots sitting under her bed. She threw the small bag over her shoulders, then changed out of the fairer, tied shoes that were more akin to hard-soled slippers than anything else before pulling on those boots. If she was going out on her own, then by the Pantheon there was no way she would do so in those worthless things. It would have been barely a step above charging barefoot into the wilderness.

With that, she was done. There were no other possessions to her name, nothing else she could take with her without stealing from the abbey. She was tempted after the public humiliation she had just suffered, but no. She refused to stoop to thievery.

Her belongings thus collected, Elya returned to the hall and left the dorms for the central courtyard and the gates that lie at its front. Huge, sturdy wooden things, she had often looked at them and wondered what the outside world had to offer her. A life of adventure did not seem so bad.

Of course, in those wonderings she had never left alone.

She crossed the courtyard, where flowers were arranged in the loamy soil of the abbey's garden, breathing in the scents of primrose, cornflower, dahlia and rose. Sunlight spilled through the open roof, warming her with its springtime heat. Home. Or at least, it had been. The gardens were her favorite place here, so it was fitting it would be the last she saw of the place.

"Ballian preserve you all, I tried..." Elya whispered. But she didn't look back again, opening the smaller door built into the gates and stepping through into the world.

Eran called. Maybe even further lands.

They whispered to her, and she wanted to see them. Though of course, the first thing she had to do was survive the coming of the Horde. A task far easier said than done.

It was about two hours into Elya's trek through the forest that she encountered her first issue.

The problem in question declared itself through the loud grumbling of her stomach. She ignored it and the beginning of hunger pangs as she pressed on, hoping some sort of solution would present itself as she traveled. She took short, careful sips of her water and maintained an easy pace to make sure she did not push herself too hard. She knew the limitations of her body, learned through a life led as a glorified servant for the Order. She was no stranger to hard work, but journeying through the wilderness was different.

As the sun began to set and the first moon, Vena, began to rise, Elya finally had to come to terms with the fact that she simply did not have the skillset to rough it in the forest on her own. If she had the time – if circumstances had been different – she would have made for the town of Talwich itself, about three miles West of the abbey. The town had been evacuated for half a month already, though, and the Horde was making its way North at an alarming rate based off the last bit of news the town had delivered.

If she wanted to live, she had to go straight North herself as quickly as possible and hopefully cross whatever border the Caldrian army was preparing to stop the barbarians from the Far South.

Which brought her to another issue: Elya had no idea how far the military border was and with the sun gone, was already beginning to grow confused about her direction. If she wound up going the wrong way in the dimmer lighting, it would only lower her chances of survival. Thankfully when the second of the Twin Moons, Vexa, joined her sister in the sky their light was able to provide enough illumination to keep her from straying far.

"Bless you, Father Ballian, for watching over me and clearing the clouds from the sky this night," she murmured. Prayer to the Father of the Hearth was a habit built through her years with the Order, and despite the failings of his followers she still somehow found comfort in seeking him on her own.

'Faith isn't subject to the whims and corruptions of mortal humanity. It's about trusting in something greater than myself and doing what feels right. Moira isn't perfect, but neither am I. but that doesn't mean I can't find comfort in my belief,' she thought firmly.

Oddly enough, in the short time since she stood up to Mother Moira and was subsequently cast out, she had never felt closer to Ballian. She had to believe all of it had happened for a reason.

Another few hours passed before the trees finally broke and Elya found herself in a small clearing, bisected by a small, babbling brook. Sighing with relief, she hurried to the edge of the water and splashed herself in the face. It was startlingly frigid, but the cold did what she needed it to and shocked her back to alertness. Filling her water bladder once more, she took a couple of sips as she considered herself in the rough reflection of the water. She could just make out her mess of thoroughly frizzed black curls, a huge poof sprouting from her head, her dark skin marred by a cut from Moira's slap beneath one of her near-gray eyes.

She scoffed, then stood and continued.

The location might have made for a good place to sleep, but one never knew what manner of creature might stumble upon you in the depths of Talvern Forest. Most of the local wildlife had fled, like they could the Horde coming the same way they fled before floods or tornadoes. Even the local monster population had gotten quiet.

It was as though the world itself knew disaster was around the corner.

Even still, it was always better to be careful and avoid surprises.

That was when she rounded a particularly large tree and stumbled over something lying on the ground. She let out a surprised shout as she fell, slamming into the trunk of the tree with her elbow and turning her ankle as her leg jerked to the side.

Then she landed on something cold and still. It took her a good few moments to realize what she was looking at, and then she had to stop herself from puking out what food had not yet passed through her stomach. Elya had landed on the corpse of a wolf, mutilated beyond belief. Her hand and knees, used to brace her fall, were now decorated with the body's sticky, congealed blood and bits of plant matter.

Its maw was open to an unnatural extent, ripped back until the top half of its skull was nearly pulled from its body.

"Blood of the Pantheon..." she whispered. Then, despite her attempts to fight it, she was sick, adding to the filth she was already sprawled across.

What happened to this poor creature?! Looking around, she realized it wasn't the only one. There was an entire pack in similarly disturbing states. It was horrible.

The bodies were not fresh, that much she could tell. It calmed her down a bit as she tried to hurry back to her feet, only to wince and lean against the tree she had slammed into before to take the weight off the hurt ankle.

"Just great..." she hissed to herself. Looking at the state she was in, Elya turned away from the dead wolves and hobbled her way back the yard or so she had walked from the clearing. She had to do an awkward sort of shuffle once she no longer had trees to support herself with, but eventually made it to the water and managed to sit without collapsing.

She was trying not to panic, but her thoughts were running rampant.

'How can I possibly move quickly enough to escape the coming of the Aarn now? How can I even keep up the easy pace I set so far? And my elbow... it's not as bad as my ankle, but it's going to bruise at a minimum...'

It was a lot. Too much.

She pulled the boot off of her wounded foot, hissing every time it jostled what she realized was a rapidly swelling ankle, then the woolen sock beneath it. Finally, she lowered the foot into the cold water and sighed in relief as it instantly went to work easing some of the pain.

Squeezing her eyes shut, Elya leaned her head back so her face was toward the sky, using both hands to keep herself balanced in the grass.

"Ballian... I know I broke one of the tenets of your Order... I know I was cast out by your faithful... but please, Father... help me," she said, her voice quiet and carried away by the breeze. She kept her eyes shut when what felt like a rush of warmth started to spread through her body, beginning in her chest. It was unlike anything she had ever felt. It felt, somehow, like coming home.

The problem was, whatever that light was that was growing brighter and brighter, its strength was burning itself into her eyes even through her eyelids. She cracked her eyes open just a bit, to see what was causing it... and her mouth fell open.

Brilliant waves of warm, golden light pulsed out from her chest, over her body and then concentrated on her ankle and elbow. With every pulse, she felt more of her pain fading away, a fresh strength replacing it as her spirit soared like it never had before. Tears sprang to her eyes and she could not stop them from falling.

Elya knew what this meant.

Anyone who ever worshipped one of the Pantheon dreamed of it. The Order of Ballian itself counted only a few dozen blessed enough among their number for it, and every single one of them was cared for as the gift from their Father that they were. Yet here she was, alone, wounded, a veritable mess and still.

Ballian had chosen her. Elya was a Font. Blessed to wield the holy power of her god, either as a Priest or a Paladin or... who knew?

As the light began to fade, the warmth of that glow receding back into the center of her chest, she worried for a moment it would leave her. Yet when it had fallen back to the point where it had begun, it stayed. Like a little, glowing ball of heat reminiscent of nights she and the other Daughters had spent huddling around the huge hearth in the dormitories during the depths of Winter.

It truly did feel like home. She had been forced to leave hers behind that very day, but Ballian refused to cut her off from his warmth. If she had doubted her choice to question, to try and ensure the lives of her family, her sisters, no more. This was proof she was right.

Which, of course, unsettled her. If she was right, then everyone who had stayed behind would be dead. The Order's tenets were wrong – or, at least, Mother Moira's interpretation of them was. If she went back, if she showed them the gift their Father had given her, would they listen? Could she save them all?

It had been weighing her down in the back of her mind since she left, a dark pit that she had refused to acknowledge or even consider at all for fear of what it might do to her when even her own life was not promised. Now? She had a chance to rescue the only family she had ever known.

Even if it did not change her circumstances, even if the Order never welcomed her back, was it not her responsibility to try?

With a fresh determination, Elya pulled her no-longer-wounded foot from the water of the brook and quickly slipped her sock and boot back on. She stood, clenching her fists as she turned and... realized she had no idea how to get back to the abbey.

A branch snapped, yanking her focus from that issue to something new.

"Well I suppose that answers my question," a voice said. A man slid down from the thick branch of one of the trees, catching himself with one arm to slow his descent before letting himself drop lightly the last two feet.

"This is when you ask, 'Oh Dorian, what question are you talking about?'" the man continued, as if his sudden entrance was a normal, everyday occurrence. He moved with a lithe, natural grace as he stepped toward her, smirking.

"Wha- ?" she tried to say, before cutting off rather lamely. "I... who... ?" she tried again, stammering like a fool as the man chuckled.

"My question! I introduced myself all dramatically talking about how my question was answered, so the obvious follow-up to that would be to ask, 'What question did I answer, Dorian?'" the man, who she assumed must be Dorian, replied, coming to a stop just a short distance away. He adjusted his bow where it was slung over his shoulder while his smirk turned into a full grin.

He was tall, at least six feet, and thin as a reed, though the sort of thin that looked like corded muscle had been stretched out across a wire frame. He had hair the color of an angry fire and bunches of freckles all over his face, but the thing that was most telling of all were his eyes. Green like the deepest forest, and full of mirth.

"Oh, wait," Dorian said, his eyes widening as though he had realized his mistake. "There's no way you could have known my name before I spoke. Hm... I guess that means the obvious follow-up question would have been, 'What question did I answer, remarkably gorgeous stranger?'"

At this, the man wiggled one of his eyebrows suggestively. It was just so wildly absurd, mere seconds after her miraculous discover, that she could not help it. Elya burst into full, belly-aching laughter, folding over her own arms as it came.

"What, was it something I said?" Dorian asked, though from his wink it was clear he knew what he was doing. Finally, after she managed to catch her breath and wiped the tears from her eyes, she stood up. Still grinning, she humored the strange man who had saved her life.

"Fine. What question did I answer for you, Dorian?" she asked, too giddy from the bout of laughter and the ridiculous nature of her day to care.

"Why, that's simple! I heard you when you took your stumble before, came rushing to make sure no one was in danger, only to find you vomiting on a wolf corpse. Bold choice, by the way. Anyways, when that happened, I had to know: are you stupid, brilliant, or out of your mind?"

Elya's brow furrowed as she considered the slightly offensive question, but she supposed she could understand why he would be wondering. The fairly manic series of emotions she had gone through in the time he had been observing her would have worried anyone.

"And the answer?" she prompted, making Dorian grin again.

"Why, all of the above, of course! Just the way I like it." At that, the man took a bow, then took her hand before she could say a thing and pressed his lips to her fingers. "Greetings, m'lady of... some church or other. Dorian Freylind, at your service. Might I know your name? It is customary to give yours when another offers theirs, after all."

Face flushing at the man's frankly absurd forwardness, Elya pulled her hand back, though not unkindly.

"Elya is my name. Just... just Elya," she managed despite the rising levels of nervousness she felt in her stomach. Dorian chuckled again and stepped back.

"Well then, 'Just Elya.' Beautiful name, that. Just Elya, I cannot help but notice that you seem to be rather confused as to where you should be heading. Could I ask what your destination might be? It seems a bit odd that a Font of any church would be wandering alone in such a state. Especially at night. Doublly especially – is that proper? - so close to the arrival of a slavering, bloodthirsty, terrifying horde of barbarian arctic bear-apes."

It took her a moment to parse through that knot of wordplay before she understood the question. She finally found herself wondering if she should tell this man anything else. After all, despite his good humor and the fact that he had saved her life, he was ultimately a stranger.

Usually it would be quite odd to be sharing things like this with a complete stranger, but...

Something inside of Elya felt like she could trust the man. It was a feeling, a... tingling? It felt like it was coming from that warmth in her chest, almost as though Ballian was trying to show her... she had no idea what. So she had to decide, and remarkably she found herself deciding rather easily.

"Well, Dorian, I came this way because this morning I was thrown out of Talwich Abbey and excommunicated from the Order of Ballian. Just because I tried to say we should leave the abbey behind and flee from the Horde you're talking about, which is against one of the tenets of the Order. As for being a Font, well..." She shrugged awkwardly, still trying to process that herself. "It's as new to me as it is to you."

Dorian's eyes slowly widened in surprise the longer that Elya spoke, until at the end he broke out into laughter.

"Those idiots refuse to leave, throw you out because you suggested it and made you an exile, only for you to suddenly discover later in the same day that you're a Font?! By the Pantheon, I wish I could see their faces if they ever find out!" he cackled. Finally he got his mirth out, the noise petering off before he continued. "Still, that makes me wonder about my question even more. Where are you going?"

Elya considered a moment before replying again, looking down at her hands as she started twiddling with her fingers, considering.

"I... I feel like it's my duty to go back to the abbey and show them. To try and convince them to leave again, now that I have proof that Ballian agrees with me," she decided to say, watching Dorian to see how he reacted to that bit of information.

For the first time he grew serious, looking at her up and down as though he was considering her anew.

"That... is a very honorable thing, Just Elya. Though unfortunately, I fear your new status wouldn't change much. Sometimes, people are just... stubborn... about their beliefs, especially when it comes to religion. No one likes to be wrong, which makes it very easy to twist whatever they need to in support of their own understanding," the man said. Elya made to speak, to try and refute him despite her own misgivings that aligned very neatly with his words, but Dorian raised a hand to head her off.

"Still, as I said, that's honorable. A choice I think that my friends may be willing to support you in, if you'd like help. If nothing else, we might be able to lend more weight to your words."

For obvious reasons, Elya was unsure of the offer. It was one thing to speak with a man and tell him where she was headed. It was another entirely to follow him Ballian-knew-where and surround herself with even more strangers.

Cautiously, she said, "Look, Dorian, I appreciate the rescue. And the laughter. The Pantheon knows I needed it. But I don't know you. How can I just blindly trust you enough to follow you to your 'friends?'"

The ranger lifted his hands placatingly, nodding before she even finished speaking.

"I get it, I do. If you want to know how you can trust me, I suppose there's no way to guarantee it. Like you said, you don't know me and you're in a very stressful situation. I don't have much I can say to convince you, but... what if I can intrigue you?"

Elya squinted at the man. "What does that even mean?" she asked.

At this, Dorian carefully set his bow on the ground and then began to roll up one of the sleeves of his long-sleeved, gray shirt.

"Intrigue. Catch your interest. Show you something that leaves you dying to know the truth," he tells her, still rolling his sleeve up, slowly as though for dramatic effect.

"I don't understand how anything you could say or do would ever be 'intriguing' enough to make me go wandering off with..."

Elya trailed off as her eyes saw the bottom of the tattoo. Dorian finished pulling his sleeve up with a jerk, and in proper dramatic fashion revealed the full image: a white silhouette of a howling wolf's head set inside a circle, with the rays of the sun emerging all around it.

She looked from the tattoo, up to Dorian's expectant face, then back to the tattoo again. She had never seen it in-person before, but that symbol was legendary and instantly recognizable. It belonged to a group whose exploits could fill half a dozen tomes and still have more to share.

"The... Sun Wolves?" she whispered, barely believing the words as they left her lips.

And Dorian, that bastard, was grinning the most frustrating of grins. Because he knew, the instant she saw it. He knew he had her. He knew she would need to see for herself if it was true.

"Abyss take you," she hissed, but Dorian only laughed.

CHAPTER TWO

"Look, all I'm saying is that it would make sense," Dorian said as he strode with more confidence than any person had a right to through the moonslit forest. Eyla sighed, having long since passed the point of tolerance for the man's seemingly unending humor.

"It's really okay, I don't care," she replied, groaning when he glanced back and chuckled.

"No, seriously!" he continued, knowing full well that she had been politely trying to stop him and not caring in the least bit. "I'm a Sun Wolf, and I just saw a bunch of dead wolves! If you wanted to ask if I'm doing okay after such a horrific ordeal, it would be completely understandable and very welcome."

Then Dorian froze, looking back at Elya with such an intense look of terror on his face that she thought something was actually wrong. Until he continued.

"Oh Pantheon, what if they were family? Were those my cousins?!"

She could not help it. Stomping up to the laughing ranger, she shoved him with all the strength she could muster and knocked him back just a little. Unphased, he kept laughing as he turned around and resumed his lead.

"What have I gotten myself into?" Elya whispered, before starting after him.

It had been maybe an hour since they met and Dorian's boundless energy was more than astonishing. He might be annoying, but the more time that she spent with him the more she came to understand that he was a good sort. Odd, maybe, but then if he was telling the truth and was a member of the Sun Wolves it had to be expected. Only oddities could cut it in a group so famous.

They went on for a short while longer, with Dorian constantly filling the empty space with one-sided conversation, when suddenly she noticed movement just as two people stepped out of hiding.

"Still can't shut that mouth of yours, huh, Dorian?" one of them said immediately, a woman with a shaved head and fabric pulled up to conceal her face. She had a hand on a small axe slipped through the loop of her belt, while a sling hung from the other at her side.

"Ah, Mara, still can't admit your attraction towards me? We've been over this! You don't have to hide behind that surly act of yours," he shot back, not missing a step while Elya had frozen in place, pulse beating like a hammer at the surprise.

"Please stop flirting with my wife, Dory," the other person, a dark-skinned man whose build was similar to Dorian's except with a more traditionally muscular tint, interjected. He too had his face concealed, with a hood up as welk. Two rather large daggers, thicker than her arm from blade to spine, were at his hips and a bow twice the size of Dorian's across his back.

Dory? She smirked a bit at the decidedly less important-sounding moniker, especially when she saw him wince at its use. The whole, rapid-fire interaction was quickly calming her back down again.

"Is that nickname necessary, Ode? My name is Dorian! It's a good, strong name, one I'm very proud of. One the ladies enjoy, too! Dory is just so... so..." Whatever else he was about to say, it was stopped when the woman made a show of wiggling her axe.

"Shut up." she growled, then turned around, dismissing him outright.

Before Dorian could reply again, the man called Ode cut him off.

"Enough, Dory. The big man was looking for you. You were supposed to report in a while ago," he said, interrupting the direction of the conversation that Dorian just seemed to naturally set. The ranger quickly sobered up, glancing back at Elya before clearing his throat and nodding.

"Yes, I... well, there was a bit of a situation and so I brought someone with me." Ode turned his gaze to Elya and took her in with the efficiency of someone well about their business.

"The tagalong, I assume?" the man said, while gesturing toward her. Realizing then that she had just been silently staring the entire time, she ignored her embarrassment and stepped forward.

"I'm sorry if I kept Dory," she said, smiling a little as Dorian winced at the nickname again.

"Just go see Morgan. Bring her along and explain. We're in the middle of an operation, so every single person in camp needs to be accounted for," Ode replied, getting a sharp nod from Dorian before he gently led Elya on.

"You ready?" Dorian asked as they left the other two behind.

"I am. I hope it's not too much to hope you all might have enough food for me to eat something?" she responded, giving him a small smile as she finished.

Her hunger might have kept her mind sharp longer than it would have been otherwise, but at this point it had to be well past midnight. Unto early morning, even. She had not eaten since breakfast the day before, nor slept since she woke the same morning.

"Oh, don't you worry about that!" the ranger exclaimed, jostling her slightly with his shoulder and grinning. "I've got you covered. You'll just need to come see someone with me first."

Elya considered.

"This Morgan person?" she inquired, more than just a bit curious. Dorian nodded, made to answer her question, then stopped himself as they passed through the trees into a massive, man-made clearing where stood an impressive encampment.

"You'll see for yourself in a few minutes, but... here we are," he finally said, running a hand through his fiery locks.

Rows of neatly ordered tents, mostly silent save for a select group of armed and armored men and women on watch, were awash with moonlight. At the center of the camp a much larger tent stood, obviously some sort of command center for this mercenary outfit, but there were plenty of mercenary groups out there.

None of that was what held her attention.

Instead, it was the banner planted before that big tent, proudly bearing the same symbol Dorian had on his arm. The howling wolf's head over black rays of sunlight, all on a field of deep orange. The Sun Wolves. Was it truly them...?

"Come on, Just Elya," Dorian began, the awful nickname pulling her focus back to the ranger, who once again was grinning. "You've got some people to meet."

The first thing that Elya noticed as she entered the well-lit commander center was the huge table at its center, a map of the area spread across its length with tons of markings covering it. It was the focal point of the entire space, with chairs on all sides. She knew nothing about strategy, but she figured it was safe to assume that the set up was for planning.

After the table, Elya found her eyes naturally moving to the far end of the tent where a group of people stood in discussion, not yet aware of the new arrivals.

"Oh good, everyone's here! Makes my life easier," Dorian declared, making her jump and getting the attention of those inside. The ranger himself strode by, headed toward the group with the same cockiness as always. Swallowing her nerves, Elya stayed close behind, trying not to be too intimidated by the new people... and they were certainly intimidating, each in their own way.

One man, gray-bearded and partially balding with the bulkiest musculature she had ever seen, stood at least six-and-a-half feet tall and was by far the largest individual present. He took in Dorian's approach before his eyes found Elya and, in stark contrast to his physicality, one of the most welcoming smiles she had ever seen split his face.

Another of the group was a young man with long, blonde hair down to his shoulders and patchy stubble growing in under a soft face and brown eyes. He wore loose clothing with leather pads of armor sewn into his shoulders and across his abdomen and back. The runic tattoos that covered his body marked him as a wizard, a true rarity even before considering the scope of his tattoos. Elya only knew the bare minimum about wizards, but that included the fact that the level of mana within their bodies influenced the density and size of their Runescript. Judging by this man's tattoos, he was very powerful indeed.

The two remaining, however, were the most striking.

First was the woman, her long, silvery hair – true silver, not gray - done up in a bun that gave a sharp definition to the strong angles of her face. She had to be in her forties at a minimum, but her beauty was unmarred by middle-age.

She was well muscled and wore a white tabard over a brown shirt and pants, a golden wolf sewn into the tabard over her chest. She was already moving to meet them, a sort of stern but caring glint to her eyes as she leveled them on Dorian.

Even as she started to speak to the ranger, though, Elya found herself turning her focus to the last person of the group. All of them had a presence, but this man was like something animalistic given human likeness.

The older man was bigger, but something about this last person was... dominating.

Cropped black hair peppered with gray and a neat beard kept close to his jaw, eyes a strange shade of green so light they seemed yellow, all over a framework of tan skin and cold surety. He was the only one in armor, armor so black it seemed as though it could be made of onyx. It gleamed in the flickering torchlight that lit the tent. His sheer intensity felt like an electric current in the room and it was all she could do to drag her attention from gaping at him back to the woman who had approached when Elya realized she had been addressed.

"Um, I'm sorry. What was that?" she replied lamely, earning a raised brow from the woman and yet another laugh from Dorian.

"I said that my name is Elaine de Lustra, that it's a pleasure to make your acquaintance, and that I was wondering how a Daughter of Ballian found her way to us with disaster so close at hand," the woman - Elaine – explained. The wizard walked up to stand next to her, an inquisitive gleam in his eyes as he looked her over more closely.

"I must confess I am similarly curious. Especially considering you are a Font. Untrained, the Mana tells me, yet still," the magic caster added. His words made the rest of them do a double take. Even Dorian looked surprised. Elya was just as shocked as the rest.

"How could you tell?" she stammered. Calling her confused would have been an understatement. The wizard shrugged.

"The Mana can sense the holy power inside you, and I can speak to the Mana. Simple communication, ma'am," he explained, before turning to the two who had not come closer.

"She's trustworthy. Certainly not a danger to any of us, and… I sense karmic bonds tethering her here. To Mr. Freylind, likely in relation to whatever business led to him bringing her along, but there is something else as well. Something older that I'm not quite able to pinpoint. Nevertheless, I sense no ill intent at all."

By the time the tattooed spellcaster finished speaking Elya felt resoundingly unnerved at being so easily read. And how could she have any sort of 'karmic connection' to these people? Whatever that even meant. At least meeting a wizard was every bit as confusing as she had always imagined it might be.

"Well ain't that interesting?" the older man practically bellowed, so loud did he speak. He scratched his thick gray beard and stepped forward, extending a hand.

"The name's Garth, miss. Garth Damassi, though 'round here most just call me Uncle Gar," the man said. Elya awkwardly raised her hand to his and goggled appreciatively when Garth's hand completely enveloped hers. Everything about him was just massive. Thankfully, that size was belied by a gentle care that showed he was not some thoughtless meathead.

"Elya. Um, j-" she paused when she caught the snicker already on its way out of Dorian's mouth, frowned and changed what she was about to say. "Elya, no family name."

Something in the room shifted, and for a moment she was not sure what had happened. Then she saw the man in black armor had taken a step forward, looking almost surprised before quickly correcting his face back to what seemed to be a customary frown. Elaine's face had changed as well, taking on a sort of contemplative distance as she turned to look at the man yet to introduce himself.

"Elya, you say? Perhaps out of Talwich Abbey? It's the only Home of the Order of Ballian for quite some distance, after all," the regal woman finally said, emphasizing the word Home in a way that any faithful of the Lord of the Hearth would understand.

"That's exactly where I came from. Though, I was… thrown out, and told in no uncertain terms I would not be welcomed back," the Font replied, though by now her eyes were moving from face to face to see if anyone would be explaining why some of them were acting so odd.

"Thrown out?"

They were the first words the armored man spoke, and his voice rumbled like a sound a beast would make, a baritone so rich it seemed to have character all its own. His eyes had narrowed the tiniest fraction, barely enough for Elya to notice. She nodded.

"Yes. They… well, the Mother there has a very particular interpretation of Ballian's Scriptures. She thinks abandoning the abbey would be a grave sin against our Lord. I argued with her, tried to convince everyone to leave before the Horde arrived and save themselves, but she called it blasphemy. It…" she had given a passing explanation to Dorian about what had happened to her, but this was the first time she had said it all fully fleshed out and she found that it hurt much more than she realized.

"So she threw you out? Knowing the danger coming this way? For *that*?" the man replied. His anger was such that it roiled through the room like a heat, an emotion so vivid Elya could feel it. She nodded, slowly, unsure what she had done to upset the man so much. His fists clenched at her confirmation. Elaine stepped over to him, taking his hands in her own and whispering quiet, soothing words while Garth stepped over to block her view.

"Sorry, miss. If'n you don't mind, let's afford'em as much privacy as we can for a few moments. Maven?" the bear of a man said, turning to look at the wizard as he finished and getting a nod in return.

He started speaking, a short sentence but in a language unlike any Elya had heard before. The words felt as though they held all the secrets of the universe, and when he finished Maven snapped a finger and a ball of silence enveloped the area directly around the whispering duo.

"Shouldn't take too long now, miss. Apologies," Garth continued. Elya just nodded. What else could she do?

Thankfully it truly did not take long, and when the two broke apart the magical silence faded with another snap of Maven's fingers. Elaine walked over, followed closely by the now much calmer man.

"Sorry. My name is Morgan, Morgan Arn Rohadi," the man said, giving Elya a nod that seemed strangely soft for someone so obviously very serious.

"Morgan and I are the commanders of this company, Elya. He is also my husband, and his apology is sincere, no matter how gruff he may appear about it. Your story simply… reminded him of someone," Elaine added, poking Morgan's side with her elbow playfully and drawing a small smile from the man.

"It's okay. It… well, I suppose it happens, doesn't it?" Elya replied, deciding that this introduction had already become awkward enough without pushing what was obviously a touchy subject. Then, as she set all that awkwardness aside, she finally had enough space in her thoughts for her brain to work properly and she started, taking a step back as she looked over the four of them with something far closer to awe than her previous examinations.

"You really are the Sun Wolves!" she exclaimed. Now that she was using the brain Ballian had blessed her with, she recognized all of their names, noticed the tattoos peeking out in different places across their bodies. Garth the Half-Giant had the symbol emerging from the top of his shirt, betraying its location on the right side of his chest. Maven – Maven the Maestro! – had it on one of his palms, which she noticed as he reached up to scratch his chin. Elaine de Lustra, the Hammer of Dawn, had it tattooed on the back of her neck, hers a more elegant, golden-inked version.

And Morgan? Morgan Arn Rohadi, by the Pantheon, the Dread Wolf himself! He had the symbol below his chin, where his neck met his jaw, blending into his beard.

"You hear that, guys? Even the Daughters of Ballian have heard of us. It's nice to be famous," Dorian suddenly added, reinserting himself into the conversation in proper dramatic fashion.

"I apologize Mr. Freylind, but due to the obvious fact that Elya is just now making her declaration after meeting the four of us, simple deduction tells us that her recognition of our company has nothing to do with you," Maven answered immediately. Dorian clutched his chest, looking so scandalized one might think a puppy had been murdered.

"I think ya hurt his feelings, Maven," Garth suggested, as he dropped a huge, meaty hand on Dorian's shoulder in what was probably an attempt to show pity but instead just looked like a threat. One which Dorian obviously knew the truth of, because he brought the back of his hand to his forehead and turned to Garth.

"You're the only one who understands me, Uncle Gar," the ranger complained. Finally, Elaine and Garth cracked, grinning at the jokes, though Maven looked confused and Morgan appeared unmoved altogether.

"Dorian's antics aside," Elaine began, righting the course of the conversation once more, "Elya, given your circumstances you are more than welcome to stay under our protection until the Aarn threat has passed. As a matter of fact, I'm going to insist on it."

She met Elaine's gaze, stunned by the offer made before she could even ask. She had hoped for something like this, but for the idea to not even come from her? She was nodding before she was conscious of it.

"I would really appreciate that, thank you!" she exclaimed, unable to hide her sheer relief. Elaine turned to Dorian, coughing lightly to get his attention.

"Dorian, I want you to take Elya back with you to meet the rest of your squad. Let her get a feel for the guild. I'll make sure a spare tent and sleeping gear is sent your way. Also, I'm assigning Asani to her with more specific instruction, so please send the Captain this way when you get there," the woman commanded. Dorian snapped off a surprisingly sharp salute before dipping into a half-bow.

"As you say, Commander," he replied, before turning to Elya and winking. "Now then, how about we go and get you that food?"

Saying the word 'food' made her stomach gurgle angrily and she blushed, nodding.

"That would be appreciated," she said, smiling sheepishly.

"Off we go, then!" Dorian declared, spinning about and heading for the tent exit.

"I want you back here with Asani, Dorian. Get Elya settled, then return. You still have a report to make," Elaine called after him. The ranger whirled, smirked and then nodded.

"Will do, ma'am," he said. Then he backed out of the tent, forcing Elya to follow quickly or be left behind. Still, the whole way out she felt Morgan's eyes following her, studying her.

She really hoped she would get answers for the strangeness with him. Having the focus of the Dread Wolf was remarkably unnerving.

Dorian led Elya at a quick trot through the camp, threading his way along what seemed to be purpose made lanes toward a section closer to where they entered the clearing. Here she found quite a few younger people around. She was not sure of Dorian's exact age, but he had to at least be near her own. Others they passed as the camp slowly began to wake for the day, the first rays of dawn poking through the trees, appeared to be of similar age as well. Perhaps the newest members of the guild had congregated to this portion of the camp?

Thankfully, the layout was not too confusing and they reached their destination swiftly. A small fire burned in the center of a ring of tents, logs arranged around to create some crude seating. Three people were already sitting around the fire with a kettle suspended over it. A strange scent, strong and sort of earthy, permeated the air while the three individuals laughed about something one of them had said.

One of them noticed Dorian approaching and pointed at him.

"Heeeey! Little Dory is back!" she shouted. The other two turned to look, as well.

"Little Dory!" they also said in unison, which was made more surreal by the fact that they were twins. The only difference between the two was that one had the right side of their head shaved, and the other had the left side shaved, each with intricate geometric tattoos on the scalp while on the other side their black hair was kept long, down to their shoulders. Both wore identical leather armor, though one had two swords strapped to his hips and the other had two wickedly fierce looking gauntlets lying on the ground next to him, obviously meant to turn a punch into something much worse.

The woman who shouted first, on the other hand, had short hair kept back in a bun, with a flanged mace hanging across the back of her hips. Her Sun Wolf tattoo was prominently displayed just above the corner of her right eye, making it even more distinct on her than on most others Elya had met.

"Ah, hah! Funny! Everyone knows you call me Little Dory because you feel deficient next to me, but it's okay. I understand. Greatness can be blinding," Dorian shot back, but then he paused in his approach and turned with a grand gesture to indicate Elya. "Alas, I would go on about my greatest virtues in detail, but this moment is not about me."

"Not about you?" snorted one of the twins, the other shaking his head.

"To think the day would come I would hear you say those words in that order. I'm impressed, Dorian," someone said from within one of the tents. A moment later, a woman with milky-pale skin and shoulder length black hair above eyes a shade of brown akin to fallen leaves in Autumn pushed aside the flap of her tent with a quick flicker of movement, joining them before the fire. She wore strange, segmented armor, with leader padding under flaps of metal that acted almost like an insect's shell from her shoulders down to her elbows, over her chest and stomach, all the way down to just above her knees. Beneath that she wore loose, poofy clothing that looked like it probably made it easier for her to move. On her hip was sheathed a strangely curved sword the likes of which Elya had never seen.

"Hey cap! Just the woman I was looking for. The big bosses want to see the both of us back at the command center soon, but first: may I introduce Just Elya! She'll be staying in camp with us 'til the Aarn have passed – please, as a favor to me, do be kind to her. She appears to be madly in love with me, and who can blame her?" Dorian replied.

Elya, by sheer reflex before she could stop herself, reached up and smacked the ranger in the back of the head.

There were several moments of stunned silence before the twins and the woman with the mace erupted into laughter, while the captain – Elya assumed she was the woman named Asani that Elaine had asked for – grinned.

"I think she'll fit right in!" guffawed one of the twins.

Dorian was rubbing at the back of his head and looking back ruefully at Elya.

"For shame," he whispered loudly, then sighed and shook his head.

"Well, let's do introductions quickly, shall we?" the captain said, gesturing to herself. "My name is Asani. You're not in my chain of command so that's all you'll ever need to call me, but if you hear Captain Sagi at any point, that's me as well."

Elya nodded. She was learning quickly that these Sun Wolves seemed to take everything in stride.

"Harn!"

"Ornn!"

The twins declared their names in unison, making it difficult for her to tell who said which name.

"And I'm Fahra, Fahra Amahdri. Pleasure to meet you, Elya," the last woman said, walking over and pulling her into a firm hug that took her by surprise.

"There are a couple more of us, out and about. You'll get the chance to meet them later, but you look like you're about to drop," Asani inserted once Fahra had backed away, winking at the confused Elya and punching Dorian in the shoulder.

The captain was right, of course. The adrenaline of survival had turned into the shock of meeting actual legends in the flesh, and this latest round of new introductions could only keep her focus for so long. Her body was on the verge of giving out.

"Could I maybe get something to eat?" Elya asked. Dorian looked scandalized.

"I told you that you would be able to eat, no? I see our relationship has already progressed to the point where you no longer trust me. How sad," the ranger shot back, mustering as much fake sorrow as he could.

"Shush, Dory. Come on Elya, we'll get you some food. We have dry rations on hand right away if you want to eat quickly and get some sleep? We'll make sure you get something warm in you once you're rested. I'm sure you've got quite the story to share if the Commanders are letting you stay with us!" Fahra replied. Stepping back to Elya's side, she led her gently by the shoulders to sit by the fire, then left for a few moments to retrieve something for her to eat. She returned with an apple and some dried jerky. It was not much, but to Elya, who had not eaten in quite a while, it was more than enough.

"Once you finish, you can knock out in my tent. I'm sure someone from requisitions will be by with one for you while you're down but there's no sense in waiting when all of us are up for the day," Asani told her, before turning back to the others. "See that she isn't disturbed. I'll be back when the Commanders are done with us. Come on, Dorian."

Scarfing down the rest of her food, Elya barely registered the second half of what the woman was saying. With the immediate need for sustenance sated, the sharp pangs of hunger went away. That had been the last thing primarily keeping her awake, and she let loose a yawn uncontrollably.

Once more, Fahra helped her, getting her to her feet and over to Asani's tent. The next few moments passed in a blur. In the end, all she knew was that she was lying on a mat with a warm blanket over her before the dark of sleep took her.

CHAPTER THREE

When Elya awoke, it was to the glorious scent and sound of something bubbling. The smell worked its way into her nostrils, the tantalizing mix of veggies, meat and some sort of herb pulling her from her dreamless slumber back into reality. Her grumbling stomach helped wrench her fully to wakefulness and she pushed off the mat she had been lying on, her blanket sliding off.

With a moment to herself, she realized that she looked like a proper mess. Her tan habit was caked in mud and other assorted stains, an unfortunate amount likely attributed to the innards of the wolf corpse she had fallen over. She cringed when she saw some of it had rubbed off on Asani's blankets.

Then she smelled herself.

"Ballian help me," Elya groaned, embarrassed for all of the human interaction she had participated in before sleeping. Which, now that she thought about sleeping, she began to wonder how long she had been out. It was still light outside, but it was impossible to tell where the sun was in the sky without going outside.

She was about to head out when she noticed a set of clean, folded clothing set just inside of the entrance flap.

There was a note in rough hand affixed to the top with a small stone. Slipping the small slip of paper free, she gave it a quick glance over.

'Clothes are for you. They aren't much, but they'll get you out of that mess you have on.' At the bottom, Fahra had signed her name. Smiling at the show of kindness, and more than grateful to be able to get out of what had essentially become filthy rags, Elya pulled the habit off. She looked it over for a moment, realizing that this would be the first time ever she wore something besides the same bland uniform required of all Daughters of Ballian. She felt a surprising amount of emotion as she set it aside.

It felt like officially letting go of the life she had known. A lot had already happened since being thrown out of the abbey, but this in particular struck her.

Grief affected everyone differently, and for every person it could strike for different reasons. For Elya, it first struck as she put down that nasty, ripped-up habit and began to dress in the simple black linens Fahra had left.

Though, even grieving she was still aware enough to be mortified she had fallen asleep with her boots on. That was just downright uncivilized.

After getting herself dressed in the new clothes – and making a mental note to ask for new socks as well, given the state of *those* – Elya stepped through the flap that was the tent's entrance and into the early evening. Her gaze immediately fell to Fahra, who was leaning forward from where she was seated on one of the logs, lazily stirring the contents of a pot that hung over their campfire with a ladle.

At the sound of Elya's exit, the woman paused and turned, a friendly smile lighting up her face upon seeing the newcomer awake.

"Hah! She lives! You slept the day away, you know. Do the clothes fit okay? I had to guess your size when I went looking, so I hope those work," Fahra started, before scooting over a bit to make room for Elya beside her.

Smiling thankfully, she plopped down with a sigh before her stomach rumbled.

"Ah, sorry..." Elya said, chuckling through the embarrassment. The other woman just waved it away.

"It's fine, don't worry. The food's almost done and the others will be back soon, so dinner will be served pretty quickly. The clothes, though?" Fahra replied, prompting her at the end as a reminder of her first question.

"They're great. Maybe just a tiny bit big, but it could just feel that way because the only clothes I've ever warn before these were those habits and... they're all the same, if that isn't a given."

The warrior nodded, her eye quirking a bit but otherwise staying quiet as she spoke.

"Well, I'm glad they're comfortable. I gotta say, I feel like *anything* else would be comfortable if that thing you had on was all you've had," she said. The words stung just a little bit, but Elya knew she did not mean anything rude by it. It was already feeling like Fahra could be a friend, if the time to develop a friendship was given to them. Ultimately, though, she had no idea how long she would be with the Sun Wolves. She was grateful for the safety they gave her with the Horde, but she was not sure how much time was left before their arrival now. With such a short time frame available to her before she would have to be on her way, Elya did not want the heartache that would come with building relationships with here only to then have to leave again.

"You're somewhere else right now, aren't you?" The question dragged her back to the moment, and she found she had been staring very intently into the flames in front of them.

She tittered nervously, a strange, high-pitched sound before she cleared her throat and got herself under control.

"Sorry. I, uh… it's just been a lot. The last couple of days, I mean," she answered lamely, rubbing one hand with her other nervously. Fahra looked at her intently, chewing on the inside of her lip.

"We heard a little bit. After the Captain got back, I mean. Not much, just enough to know you've been through a lot. Captain Sagi wanted to make sure you had the freedom to share what you wanted, when you were comfortable enough to do so. Even has Dorian on a short leash about it, which I'm sure you can tell already is fairly miraculous."

Elya looked over at her, smiling at the mention of Dorian.

"Yeah, Dorian is… well, is he always like that?" she asked, getting a good laugh out of her companion.

"Little Dory is a lot, but he does have a serious side to him. When things go bad, he's someone you want watching your back, no doubt about it. If you spend enough time around us, you'll see what I mean," Fahra replied, gesturing to the camp in general.

Elya's smile faltered.

"I appreciate you all being so kind to me. Everyone here has been," she paused for a moment, her lips twisting downward in a frown.

"I'm really grateful for the kindness. But I don't know how long I'm going to be here, so to make friends and then have to leave it behind would be awful."

"And you want to avoid the hurt of that happening, after losing what you had before?" Fahra inquired. Elya nodded.

"Exactly."

"Look, I get it. Trust me, I really do. No one who has joined up with 'the Sun Wolves' has led an easy or even normal life," Fahra started up after a few seconds of quiet, emphasizing the name of the company as she said it. "I've learned that if there's anything you can expect in life, it's the unexpected. Don't turn down the chance to befriend someone just because you're afraid of having to leave. Things have a way of working out in the most bizarre ways sometimes – and sometimes they don't. That doesn't mean you don't give the good a chance. It just means life is a mixed bag, and you get what you get. Good, bad, and all that stuff in between."

They were silent a long time after that, Fahra content to let Elya think as the food in the pot – a stew – continued to cook while she stirred. Maybe ten minutes of that comfortable silence passed, life continuing in the camp around them as conversation and other assorted noises rose into the air. It was finally broken by the crunch of approaching boots. When she glanced up, she saw Asani approaching.

"Good, you're up," the captain said, coming to a stop and resting a hand on the hilt of her blade in what Elya could immediately tell was a stance of habit.

"Evening, captain," Fahra put in, getting a nod from Asani before she turned her attention back to her.

"Your tent and other basic supplies were delivered while you were resting. That bundle there." As she spoke, she pointed over to the side of their circle of tents, where a bag that looked like it contained several different pieces of gear and equipment wrapped in tarp and a blanket, all bound by taut lines of twine, sat leaning against a stack of crates. "After dinner we can assist you with getting your tent set up, if you haven't put one together before. I will not be sharing any personal details related to your arrival here unless you've given allowance for it, but I'm going to relay the conditions of your stay now. Alright?"

Elya shifted where she sat, leaning back so she was sitting up straight. She did not mind if Fahra heard this.

"Sure," she said. Asani wasted no time.

"First: during your stay with the Sun Wolves, I – and my squad – will be responsible for your safety. That means that one of us will be with you at all times. I ask that if one of us tells you to do something, you do it without argument. I promise that there will always be a good reason for it."

Asani paused, until Elya realized she was waiting for a response and gave a quick nod.

"Good. Okay, secondly, Commander Rohadi has a special condition for your stay here. If you're going to be under our protection, he would like to ensure that our investment doesn't go and get itself killed somehow after the fact. That means that for the two days left before the Horde reaches this area, I will be running you through the most basic of basics with the sword. The Commander wanted me to tell you that this is not up for debate, though ultimately what you get out so little training will be completely up to you and your own ability."

This second condition was much more surprising to Elya, though she did her best to keep the confusion off her face. The fact that it came straight from Morgan himself said that he was even more interested in her survival than she thought. It was a reminder just how strange a good portion of her interactions with Garth, Maven and the Commanders had been. She already had a lot on her plate for the short time she was going to be here, but finding out what was going on with that had to remain a priority. For her own rapidly rising curiosity, if nothing else.

"That's fine. Great, even," Elya told Asani, and she meant it. If she knew how to fight, even a little, it would go a long way with keeping her alive once she was alone again. Even without the unique and extra deadly problem of the Aarn, travel through Eran and, she assumed, the other continents was full of danger. Learning how to protect herself, as well as learning more about her abilities as a Font and how to train with them, were of the utmost importance.

"I'm glad to hear that," the captain replied. It was obvious the easy acceptance was not what she had been expecting, though she seemed happy about it.

"Ah! Boys, you're back!" Fahra exclaimed, turning attention away from the conversation between Elya and Asani over to the twins and another person she had not met yet.

"El's awake!" Harn – or was it Ornn? – cried, while the other brother shoved the new person with a grin.

"Told you," he snickered.

"Seriously? How could I believe that Dorian brought a woman to camp with mortal danger so close?!" the new guy complained, turning red as he looked between the twins then over at Elya. She crooked an eye and frowned.

"I don't know you, but I'm not some catch that Dorian made. He brought me here to save my life, but I'm not… 'his.'" she shot back. Both twins looked away in a quick attempt to hide their grins, while the new person looked down at his feet and froze. Great. Did all the men here think they were the funniest people alive?

"S-sorry, I didn't mean to…" the newcomer started to say, awkwardly stammering off. On closer examination, she realized he was young. Younger than her, even, somewhere around nineteen or twenty if she had to guess. He wore his light brown hair short and cropped, and stubble grew in patches along his jawline beneath eyes of hazel. To see someone so young in a mercenary outfit of any kind, even the Sun Wolves, unsettled her, though she knew she had no right to feel that way.

"You should have known better than to trust anything these two have to say about Dorian that isn't a joke at his expense," Asani interjected, a mix of wry humor and disbelief on her face as she shook her head. Then her eyes narrowed and turned to the twins. "And you two. Go get Dorian and Riley before I decide to have you start mucking out the latrines."

That got them moving, smiles replaced with alarm.

"Yes, Captain!" they both proclaimed before running away, leaving the younger guy whose name she still did not know standing there alone.

"Come now, Luce. The longer you stand there, the weirder you'll feel. Just get the bowls and start passing them out," Fahra finally said, giving the poor guy an out. He jerked into movement, nodding to the woman before hurrying over to the crates Elya's pack leaned against. He pulled out a stack of wooden bowls and spoons then came back, setting them out in a circle around the fire while giving them directly to those who were already there.

As he came to Elya, he spoke quietly so only she could hear.

"I really am sorry." He looked so bashful about it that she reached out a hand and set it on his shoulder.

"It's okay, it's not really your fault and I didn't need to be so defensive about it," she whispered back, smiling at him. He smiled back, a wide thing that practically split his youthful face in two.

"I'm Lucem. Lucem Hallenti. But everyone just calls me Luce," he said, louder this time now that he had a bit of confidence back.

"You might have heard someone say it already, but I'm Elya. It's nice to meet you, Luce."

After their brief but welcome exchange, Elya was left with a bowl, a spoon, and that happy feeling that comes from resolving a dispute, no matter how minor.

"There's no sense in waiting around for the rest of them before we start. Help yourselves, everyone," Asani declared, once those present had settled. Luce had taken up the spot on the other side of Elya from Fahra, seeming eager to participate in the conversation now that he knew she was not angry with him.

Once they had each spooned some of the stew into their bowls, they dug in, the dull clanking of wooden utensils only occasionally broken by an exclamation of enjoyment or a wayward comment. Elya was starving for obvious reasons, but it seemed that the life of a mercenary made for some hungry individuals.

She was finishing her own food when the twins returned, Dorian and the last person she had yet to meet in tow.

"Ah good! Elya, my dear, I know your feelings for me may be strong, but it's time you knew. This is my dearly beloved, whose seniority in her love for me places her ahead of you I am afraid! Ri-" Dorian began immediately upon seeing her, only to be shoved from behind so hard that he was thrown from his feet before hitting the ground hard. He lay there, stunned, for a few seconds before righting himself and dusting off his clothes as though nothing had happened.

"Riley, this is Elya! Elya, Riley Tamdautr!" he continued, pointing back and forth as he spoke. The woman in question rolled her eyes and stepped around him. Elya looked up. And up. And quickly realized this was by far the tallest woman she had ever seen, almost as tall as Garth, which was more than a little shocking. She looked maybe an inch or two shorter than that giant, and she held a spear over her shoulders, arms slung over the top of the shaft. She had long, plaited blonde hair that fell to her waist, and she was bound with tight muscle that put all but the burliest of men to shame.

"I'll squash you, Dory," Riley told him, then walked over and sat across the fire from Elya, giving her a little nod of acknowledgement before filling her bowl and beginning to eat.

"It's a pleasure," Elya said aloud, feeling like she should say *something,* but that nod seemed to be the giant woman's limit for conversation. Thankfully, she was saved from having to rescue the moment by Asani, who had remained standing while she ate and now came forward to set her bowl near the fire. Fahra added hers, then Luce, beginning a stack. Elya added hers as well while Asani moved to where she would be able to turn and face the whole group.

"So," she began, locking eyes with Elya. "You've now met the entirety of our squad. We're called the Fangs, and as an official announcement to everyone here, Elya is under our protection until the Horde has passed. One of us will always remain with her, so long as the threat remains, and it's not up for discussion if any of you have an issue with that for any reason."

The woman was in full 'Captain' mode by this point, so her squad members reacted as such. They all stood or sat at attention, none of them speaking up to voice dissent.

"Good. Let's all do our best to make sure she feels welcome among here for the duration of her stay. We won't have another rumor started because someone feels the need to relentlessly flirt even when the target of said flirtation has repeatedly shown disinterest," Asani continued, turning to glare directly at Dorian who had the gall to hold a hand to his chest and gasp.

"Never!" he proclaimed. "Who would dare act so dastardly when the great Dorian is around?!"

Asani, however, was having none of it.

"I swear by the blood of the Pantheon, Dorian. You have gotten us thrown out of cities and towns by the local guard far too often for me not to beat this point into your head. Leave. Elya. Alone. Understood?"

Finally, Dorian looked as though he was taking the warning seriously as he looked down at the ground. He scratched his chin absentmindedly before answering.

"Understood, captain," he said morosely. Satisfied that he was suitably chastened, Asani turned her gaze back to Elya, nodding to her.

"All of that being said, Elya, are you ready for your first lesson with the blade?" she asked. She stood before she realized what she was doing, a bead of excitement threaded into her pulse.

"Absolutely," Elya replied. Asani nodded approvingly, striding over to the side of her tent where something long was wrapped in dense fabric and bound shut with a leather strap. She picked it up, then turned and motioned for her to follow.

"Come on, then. Time is precious, and we have little enough of it already to teach you something worthwhile."

Elya nodded and jogged after the captain, leaving the rest of the squad to watch after them until they were out of sight.

"Poor girl," Ornn sighed. Harn nodded in agreement.

"She has no idea what she's getting into," Riley said, shrugging before tucking into a second helping of the stew. The others assented.

"Captain Sagi is scary," Lucem whispered.

"Again!" Asani shouted, the flat of her wooden practice blade pulling away from Elya's throat as the woman panted on the ground, the sting of yet another blow burning across the back of her legs. Aches and lines of pain covered her all over. She knew without a doubt there would be bruises, but still she she got back to her feet, steadying herself and bringing her practice sword up at the ready.

The wrapped object – objects, as it turned out – that Asani had given her had been what she called a bastard sword and a wooden practice blade of the same size. Now, her new weapon sat off to the side of the flattened sparring ground the company had cleared out in their encampment, resting in its scabbard and watched over by Garth, who apparently oversaw the training and implementation of new members to the guild, among other things.

When the Half-Giant himself had shown up to watch Elya's first training session, she had felt the tension in her body racket up to an even higher level than her nerves alone were capable of. It was *the* Garth Damassi, after all! To have him scrutinizing her every mistake was a distraction, yet she did not want to allow that to affect the outcome of this session and so was doing her best to ignore everything but the wooden blade in her hands and the one her opponent was wielding.

"Hah!" Elya found herself shouting, as Asani signaled for her to begin with a curt nod.

She ran forward, feeling the pain in her body and using it to hone her focus to the best of her ability. She came in low, practice blade coming up in an arc to catch Asani in her arm and possibly knock her weapon from her hand. The Captain twisted, her own blade flying up point first in a jab that took Elya directly in the stomach. The air blasted from her lungs, and she jerked back in a stumble.

"You threw way too much into your opening swing and left yourself open to retaliation. Sloppy. Again!" the swordswoman barked, backing away and falling into the same starting stance she took every time.

Elya hissed in pain. That jab had taken her in a rib, and she cringed with every breath. Still, though, she took a few steps back and reset. She gripped her wooden sword with both hands, trying to mimic her opponent. They had been at this for maybe an hour, the sun now almost completely hidden beyond the horizon. Torches had been lit along the edges of the sparring ground so that it was still bright enough for those making use of it.

While she and Asani had been given a decent amount of space in one corner, the rest of the grounds were still in heavy use. With conflict right around the corner, everyone seemed to be taking all the time they needed to stay ready.

Asani nodded and Elya's focus snapped back to the sword in her hands and the foe in front of her. She had not landed a single strike yet. That would change. It had to.

Gritting her teeth, she charged again. This time, she kept her sword in the ready position, then side-stepped a lazy swing from Asani at the last moment. Bringing her own wooden blade out to her left, she kept it going up until she could swing it straight down. This time the strike had some weight to it, and she was hopeful that it would land. Yet the captain was like water, simply flowing around every move she made.

In this case, she brought her weapon up in an angled guard that sent Elya's blade skittering off to the side. Then she stepped in, blade whipping around to slice down at an angle opposite to her guard.

She knew that if she stayed planted that return swing would hit her, so she did the only other thing she thought to: she threw all of her weight after her sword, narrowly avoiding a blow that would have caught her in the shoulder. Elya hit the ground hard, rolled and tried to get back up as quickly as possible – only for Asani to come in with a twirl of her weapon that would have cracked her across the face if she had not stopped it at the last moment.

"Better," the woman said, and for a moment Elya was not sure if she had heard her correctly. Then her face split in a grin as she collapsed to her rear on the ground, leaning her head back and breathing heavily.

It was the first compliment that she had gotten.

"I did not say you could take a break. Up, let's go," Asani reprimanded, and so it was straight back to business.

Elya did not know how long they went on like that, only that the first moon was already halfway into the sky and the second had just come into view when they finally slowed down.

"Enough, Elya. That's enough," the captain announced, which in turn meant Elya could spin to where she had left her things by Garth. She stumbled that direction and pulled her water bladder free with trembling fingers after dropping the wooden blade. Her fingers were beat up the same as the rest of her body, even a little bloody from the force of the wooden hilt digging into her hands during the long series of spars.

The lukewarm water still felt like a blessing straight from the hands of Ballian as it soothed her parched throat. Only after several long seconds did she pause, feeling at last like she could speak again without vomiting. Which she had already done once that night and had no desire to repeat.

"Ya did good, lil' miss!" Garth proclaimed, grinning widely down at Elya.

"Really? Because it feels like I just had my butt handed to me, repeatedly," she groaned, her tongue loosened as she winced at the thought of all the damage her body had sustained from this bout of 'training.'

"It's the best way to learn in a short period of time. Usually there would be a whole lot of introductory lessons before I allowed you to start sparring, but... like I said earlier, we don't have a lot of time," Asani explained as she, too, approached, pulling free a canteen from somewhere on her person and taking a small drink. She was winded, at least, if nothing else.

"Hopefully ya aren't too tired now, if'n you're gonna make it t'see Elaine," Garth continued, laughing loudly and jostling Elya good-naturedly. His words held her attention more than the movement, however, as she looked wide-eyed from Garth to Asani and back again.

The Captain at least looked as surprised to hear this as Elya did, looking at the old man with all the evident confusion she needed to know it was news to her.

"I'm sorry, but what?" Elya finally asked.

"She's far too exhausted to enter another training session tonight, let alone with Commander Lustra," Asani said almost at the same time. She glanced Asani's way, appreciating the support considering how slow her brain was moving in her exhaustion.

"Oh, y'all have nothin' to worry 'bout. She won't be trainin' the body, Asani," Garth replied, before turning to look Elya right in the eyes. "Elaine is a Paladin, missy. A Font, just like you, if'n a good bit further along on that path."

Eyes widening, she looked at Asani again.

"Seriously?!" she asked, the excitement of this news pushing some of her weariness away. One of the biggest problems with being a Font was that there were so few of them around that it was difficult to train new ones as they were discovered. That often made it a sort of guessing game as a Font progressed in their development. The rare few that were able to study under a teacher, even teachers wielding the power of different deities, had an incredible advantage that could push them years ahead.

The Captain smiled and nodded.

"It's been so long since I've seen the Commanders in action that the thought hadn't occurred to me before now. Yes, Commander Lustra is a Font, and a powerful one at that," Asani assured her, and Elya's excitement leapt to new heights as she pushed to her feet. Of course, her body was not happy with that and she nearly toppled over. She might have done so if a massive hand had not steadied her.

"Best get on over while ya can, El. This'll probably help ya with yer exhaustion, too," said the Half-Giant, smiling the kind of warm smile only given to those who reached a certain age. Elya nodded, a small smile touching her lips at the use of a nickname before she refocused, picking up her training blade and her true weapon which was still sheathed.

"Where is she waiting for me?" she asked while reattaching her scabbard to the belt it had come with. Garth turned and used a thumb to point toward the command tent.

"Same place ya saw 'er last. Though, my understandin' is that she'll take ya somewhere private for yer actual teachin'," he answered. Without hesitation Elya was off, not at a run but at the briskest walk she could manage with her weariness and rapidly forming bruises.

The Captain herself followed quickly behind, fully intent on keeping the young woman within her sight at all times as per the orders of the very same woman they now went to see.

Garth smiled after them, wondering how long the Commanders would go before they were unable to withhold the truth from the lass. Hopefully not too long. He was becoming fond of her very quickly.

CHAPTER FOUR

Elya found the Dawn's First Light waiting for her just outside of the Sun Wolves' command tent, eyes following the trace of the twin moons through the sky. Their glows – one a faint blue, the other a verdant green - intermixed in a beam that bathed Elaine in their light, and she stood soaking it in.

"Good, you're here," she said before Elya could speak up, Elaine's eyes snapping open as she turned to face her. She smiled, her left hand rising to rest on the haft of a one-handed hammer that was now slung at her hip. She was armored, unlike the first time they had met, her tabard with her symbol resting over plate that shone so clearly it matched the silver of her hair. Beautiful etchings that looked like something akin to Runescript covered the armor in swirling curves and patterns that were almost dizzying to look at. To complete the attire she had a large, rounded shield on her back that was maybe a third of her size and had the same etchings along its banded rim.

"Yes, ma'am - I, er, is ma'am correct?" Elya replied, cursing herself a fool for the inadequacy of her words. How she had missed it when they met she had no idea. This woman was every inch the imagination's picture of a

Paladin. It was in her confident posture, the way her eyes shown with a light that was more than just reflection.

Now, being aware of Elaine's true nature, Elya found that she felt wholly inadequate to stand before a true champion of the Pantheon. The Paladin laughed, and it was like the tinkle of bells.

"Just Elaine is still fine. You aren't one of my subordinates, and as a fellow Font if anything you're nearer to an equal – or might be, anyways, should you hold yourself to training and to the strength of your deity. Ballian is a kind god, after all, as well as one of the Secondborn. He will reward hard work and common decency well," the woman replied, before turning her focus to Asani. The Captain saluted.

"Commander," Asani said, holding her position until Elaine gestured, then fell into a more comfortable stance.

"Thank you for escorting Elya here, Captain. I see you are, as always, giving your all to your duties. It's appreciated," the Paladin told her, and Captain Sagi could not contain the satisfied smile that crept up on her face. "That being said, you may retire for the night. Matters of gods and belief are a private affair, and walking the path of a Font often leads one to face uncomfortably personal truths. I would allow Elya the opportunity to do so with as few witnesses as possible."

"Of course, Commander. She will not be needing an escort afterwards... ?" Asani inquired. Elaine shook her head, turning her gaze back to the younger woman who looked very much like a frightened deer in that moment.

"No. I will escort her back myself."

If Asani was confused by this, she did not show it. Instead, she gave another salute before turning to Elya and nodding to her.

"You are strong, I can tell that much already. Lean on that and you'll be fine," the Captain told her. Then she was walking away, slipping through the much-quieted camp back in the direction of her squad's tents and leaving the two Fonts alone.

"Well, there's no sense in delaying things. Come with me, Elya. Let us speak somewhere a bit more private," Elaine declared, turning and moving away from the command center in the opposite direction that Asani had gone. The large tent was still well lit inside, as it had been the night before, and she could hear the voices of people inside. It was likely the one place that was unendingly busy.

She took off after the Paladin, ignoring the aches and exhaustion that tried to distract her.

Before long the two of them were left the encampment entirely, walking across the open space of the clearing before entering the tree line. They passed a patrol that did not stop them or even so much as acknowledge their passing besides quickly saluting the Commander as she went by.

Soon it was just the two of them, lit only by the occasional light of the moons that made it through the quickly tightening canopy. Elya had just begun to wonder how far they were going to go from the camp before they passed through a particularly dense set of trees and found themselves before a small pond, a tiny stream of water running in from one direction and exiting out the other end.

The trees still came in tight around the little body of water, but its presence created just enough space that the two of them could do... whatever it was Elaine was about to have her do.

"So, um, why exactly are we all the way out here?" Elya asked, taking in the serene setting with a small smile despite her confusion.

"I found this place when we first set up camp, two weeks ago. It helps to have a place to go to that's quiet, where you can center yourself," the Paladin explained, still turned away as she, too, took in the sight. Then she spun, some distant emotion on her face as she looked at Elya.

"When we are what we are, it's important to be able to do that. Center yourself, I mean. It's the only way to reliably reach a state deep enough within to commune with our god and the power he or she has given us."

Elaine grinned, raising a hand as light erupted from the center of her chest, flowing down her arm until it began to rise from her fingers and palm to create a floating orb that lit up the night so brightly it seemed like dawn had come. Elya threw her hands up, trying to protect her eyes as she squinted. She could barely make out the shape of the Commander, that brilliance almost acting like a physical presence.

"I am a Font of Syranna, Goddess of the Rising Sun. A sister to your Ballian, as a matter of fact, which will help us here seeing as many of her Evocations will be similar to those you are able to call upon. Though, not completely the same." The Paladin paused long enough to close her hand and reabsorb the orb that had formed over it. With it went that blinding light, allowing Elya to see again.

"I didn't even know there were differences between the spells Fonts could use depending on their deity," she replied, wanting to show the older woman that she was an eager student. Elaine chuckled.

"The fact that you called our Evocations 'spells' tells me enough," Elaine told her. She felt her cheeks run hot.

"They're not spells?" she asked. The Paladin shook her head.

"They're not. Spellcraft is about Mana – how much a person can hold inside of them, how well they can wield it on their own through study and practice. Maven is a prime example of someone who has taken spells and brought them to their most wondrous heights. There are those in the world greater than him, but they are few and growing fewer still as time goes on."

Once more, Elaine called on her power and light emanated from her chest, this time releasing from her hand as a sort of vapor that floated through the air toward Elya. It clung to her frame like dew, then began to absorb into her body. With a start, she felt her exhaustion and pain begin to ebb away, as though someone was draining it from her body. It felt similar to what she had done to heal herself using the power of Ballian, but...

"I can see by the frown on your face you've already noticed. Good," Elaine said, before continuing. "As Fonts, we are capable of Evoking the power of our deities to perform great acts. Miracles, as those without true understanding call them. Evocations – not spells – rely on our connection with our patron or matron deity and the holy power they have granted to us. Also unlike Wizards, as Fonts we are limited in scope by the domain of our god or goddess. Healing is a near universal gift of any who serve one of the Pantheon, as the Pantheon is ultimately devoted to life and its preservation. Even if those who make up its body go about that goal in vastly different ways."

By this point Elya felt completely whole. She grinned at the renewed vigor she felt in her body. She went through the motions of a few different stretches just to feel it out and could not help but laugh. It was more than just healing. It felt like the strain her body had been through over the last days, perhaps even longer, was just gone.

"How?" she asked, amazed. Elaine was smiling back as she answered.

"As the Goddess of the Rising Sun, Syranna's healing touch renews the body like the Sun renews our world with its rise every morning. When the day comes, night fades. In this case, when her healing falls on you, the aches and pains your body feels fade completely, as the rising sun beats back the darkness."

Something inside of Elya resonated with what Elaine was telling her, something at the core of her – she even felt that ever present warmth in her chest, which had still not left her since that moment before the wolves came, begin to grow stronger.

"Then, Ballian's healing felt different because..." she began, looking down at her hands as that warmth suffused her whole body.

"Because he is the God of the Hearth. Of home, and family. While I've never met one of his Fonts, I could imagine his healing would feel very different from Syranna's. More like-"

"Coming in out of the cold and growing warm by the fire."

The words sprung unbidden to Elya's lips, and with a flash that warmth within her sparked to life without. It filled the small clearing the same that Syranna's light through the hands of Elaine had, except this felt different. It was bright, but not blinding; it threw off the cold of the night, filling the space it touched with a comfortable heat that brought tears to her eyes.

I AM HERE, CHILD. I AM ALWAYS HERE.

The words filled her mind with their enormity, enveloping her in a love she had never experienced before. The tears that had yet to fall began to stream down her face, and she laughed. Joy filled her to bursting, even as she felt the warmth begin to fade, the light receding until it eventually ceased its emanation entirely. Yet still she felt it in her chest, where she knew without a doubt it would never disappear.

Silence reigned for a long time as Elya tried to catch her breath, to recover from the wonder she had just experienced. By the time she was able to pull herself together, she looked up to see even the Paladin staring, the remnants of her own tears still on her face.

Seeing Elya look her way seemed to snap the older woman out of her reverie, and she quickly wiped at her face.

"Syranna's light, that was beautiful," Elaine chuckled. "I've met a few other Fonts in my day, but... none of their Evocations felt like *that*. What a blessing to be given."

She could only grin. The right words seemed to be eluding her. Then Elaine's face twisted in a more determined smile.

"Well, we know your connection with Ballian is strong already. That's good. Our bond with our deities can be strengthened over time, but seeing as the Horde is as close as it is, I'm going to focus more on Evocations for now. Sound alright?" the Sun Wolf Commander asked. Elya clenched her hands into fists, looking up at the sky.

"Thank you, Ballian," she whispered, before looking back down at Elaine and nodding. The Paladin placed a hand on the head of her hammer, sliding it from the loop that held it in place on her hip and closing her eyes as she dropped her grip down to the haft.

"Then let's begin," she said.

More hours passed, some of it spent learning how to channel the holy might of Ballian through her new sword, while other portions were spent in quiet contemplation as she sought to understand her Lord's power. What it was capable of. What it was not.

She managed to comprehend one Evocation in that time – she could channel the heat of a raging hearth into the swing of her sword. It turned the blade a bright orange the longer she channeled it, slowing amping up the heat. Yet the power of the Evocation kept the weapon from losing its form.

Elaine understood that one. She said it was a common Evocation for those who walked the path of a Paladin –

Blessed Weapon. It adapted a portion of a deity's domain and channeled that into a weapon of the user's choice.

For Ballian's version, it channeled the raging heat of an abandoned hearth, left to burn itself out on the bones of the home it once warmed. That exact image, those feelings and impressions, flooded her brain when she called it forth. A fury had formed in her, holy and wrathful, and Elaine needed to help calm her down before she unleashed that fury on the forest around them.

"It happens," the Paladin had told her, waving off her apology. "Evocations carry with them the weight of the emotions our deities feel when accessing the portions of their domain that feed them. It's a lot even once you're used to it, and the first time is always the most intense."

Things continued after that, the hours pouring by until once more dawn was peeking over the horizon. Its light startled Elya from a place of deep concentration. It took her a couple of minutes to return from the deep, meditative state she had been in as she once more dove into her Holy Core, that heat centered in her chest given a name by Elaine. Once she realized what she was seeing, she bolted upright.

"It's morning?! How! Ballian help me, there's too much to do. I'm going to be exhausted all day!" Elya moaned, trying her very best not to sound like a complainer and failing miserably. Her teacher laughed, standing up herself from where she had been sitting, cross-legged, just before the edge of the pond.

"Relax, Elya. My goddess is master of the dawn, or did you forget?" the Paladin said, before resting a hand on her shoulder. "Repeatedly drawing on our Holy Core like we have been can have repercussions, but we barely did much more than explore. You drew on your power a few times, true, but it should not yet strain your spirit as it would if you were truly spent. And as for your physical exhaustion, as I said..."

Light surged once again from Elaine's chest, flowing up her arm and into Elya where her hand touched her. The grogginess that had suddenly snapped into awareness once she was out of communion with her Core and Ballian rapidly faded.

"Syranna's domain includes all that comes with the morning, including waking rested from a good night's sleep as part of the cycle of renewal." She pulled her hand away once the flood of light had dissipated.

"Using her power for that too often is dangerous – nothing fully replaces a body's need for a good night's sleep – but you should be good for today alone. With today being the last day before the arrival of the Aarn, I assure you personally that you will get a good night of rest tonight."

"Wow," Elya managed. All of this, her new abilities as a Font and the chance to learn from another when so few were ever given that chance, was nearly overwhelming. Would have been, if not for the pressing danger now as close as the next day. And…

With all that she had discovered about herself, with what she felt last night, she knew she needed to do something.

"Can I speak with you and Commander Rohadi?" she asked, turning to look Elaine in the eyes as she said it. She wanted the seriousness of her request to be without question. It was obvious that the Paladin could sense that sincerity, meeting her determination with curiosity.

"That shouldn't be an issue," Elaine replied, after a moment of contemplation. A smile quirked the ends of her mouth. "I'm sure you've got something interesting to discuss. He always did."

The choice of words brought Elya pause for a moment, drew her from determination to a question.

"He? Who's 'he?'"

Elaine sighed, brushed a strand of loose hair back behind her ear.

"Someone I used to know. Someone you remind me of. Don't let my reminiscence distract you – I'll lead the way back. I'm looking forward to hearing what you have to say," she answered. Then she strode past Elya, one question answered in a way, while leaving her with many more. Yet the pressing nature of their situation pushed her to set those further questions aside.

It was time to make a request.

Their trek back to camp was quick, matching Elya's racing heartbeat. Not that Elaine sped on her way – she seemed eternally even-tempered, as though nothing could break her calm, save the touch of an actual deity as she had seen firsthand. No, it was simply that her mind was so consumed with how she might win over the two Commanders of the Sun Wolves to the task she envisioned that the time it took to get back was a blur.

Once more, the hustle and bustle of the Sun Wolf encampment in the morning filled the air, though Elya noted an undercurrent of something new this morning that she struggled to place until the third argument broke out, forcing Elaine to interfere, and she realized what it was.

Tension.

It seemed even the Sun Wolves were human in the face of an Aarn Horde.

"Sorry about that. A lot of the young ones can still get quite tense the day before a major conflict, and I'd be lying if I said it wasn't the same even for some of us more experienced folk," Elaine explained, once she had set that particularly nasty argument straight. "We do what we can to help, but with so many of us together for such a big threat, well... sometimes we can only stop the fight, instead of preventing it."

Elya did not know the first thing about running a company of mercenaries and so was more than happy to trust that the other woman knew what she was doing.

"It's fine," she said aloud, a verbal assent to placate Elaine. Not that she needed reassurance. She was already moving on, and Elya had to kick up her speed to catch back up.

It was not much longer before they reached the center of camp and the command center located there. Guards were stationed out front, as normal, though voices could be heard within. Not raised, not quite, but certainly firmer than she had heard the last time she was present with the Sun Wolves' central figures.

Elaine strode right on in, forcing Elya to sweep in on her heels to make her entrance the least amount of awkward possible. The two Fonts found a room packed with not only Morgan, Garth and Maven, but also what Elya assumed once she saw Asani present had to be all of the camp's Captains.

The arrival of the Wolves' second, more vocal and front-facing Commander brought instant silence to the room as she walked through the press. The Captains parted easily around her, giving her a straight shot to Morgan. She only paused once to wave Elya after her when she realized the younger woman had frozen at the tent's entrance, once more forcing her into action as eyes found her from every direction. She did a bit of a running-walk to catch up to her teacher, grateful when their horribly blatant entrance to what had obviously been an important moment finally ended. Elaine cleared her throat loudly enough for everyone to hear.

"Well, don't stop on my account. What were we discussing?" she inquired. Voices rose from the Captains all at once. From what Elya could tell, they were asking questions about defenses, timeline... a ton of things she had no context to even try and approximate an understanding for.

The Paladin smiled, a small thing as she turned and winked at Elya – drawing a surprised glance from Morgan at the obvious gesture of closeness – before raising one hand, the room going quiet immediately.

"One at a time, and questions and requests will be answered in the order they are received," Elaine elaborated, something about the way she said it making Elya feel almost queasy. Hands shot up, people eager to be heard. Elaine looked over them all before continuing.

"As it so happens, there is already a question pending for myself and Commander Rohadi," the woman said, drawing confused looks and irritated calls from the mercenaries before she turned to look at Elya.

"So then, what did you wish to ask?"

The words cut the breath from her lungs. If there was anyone who had not noticed her before, that was certainly no longer the case. She could feel every single eye in the huge tent trained on her and groaned.

Why did it have to happen this way?

Elya stammered, tried to say something. Anything. Anything to look less like the fool that she was. That failed long enough that Elaine, looking thoroughly amused, prompted her again before pulled her over to stand next to the Paladin in a more prominent position. Directly between Elaine and Maven, who as seemed quite bored with the proceedings.

She began to panic. Then she remembered Ballian's warmth, his words to her last night: she was not alone.

"Um, hello," Elya began, looking out at the faces in front of her. Skilled warriors and, she had to assume, leaders all, to be Captains among such legendary figures. Yet here she was, about to ask a dangerous favor not only of their Commanders as she had intended, but now of all of them. She gritted her teeth. Pushed on.

"I wanted..." She cleared her throat. "I wanted to request the aid of the Sun Wolves. I do not have anything in the way of money or reward, save hopefully the satisfaction of saving lives... but I ask anyways. Please, help me to save the Daughters of Ballian at Talwich Abbey. My sisters."

Elya's words met silence first, each person standing now with more than just confusion on their faces – though she could not tell what else they might have been feeling for the pounding of her heart.

Yet if the captains were yet unsure how to respond, another standing nearby had no such problem.

"I see zero reason why we should take such a random and highly dangerous course of action for someone we barely know," Maven said, the Wizard barely glancing her direction as he spoke. Elya felt the sting of his words, even knowing there was no way her request had a chance at making it through without drawing some resistance.

She girded herself – a deep breath in, a deep breath out. Then she met the Wizard's gaze. Up this close, the tattoos were even more intimidating, but those eyes? They were boring into Elya like he saw everything that she was, everything she could possibly be... she gritted her teeth, continued.

"I know you don't really know me. Most of you even in passing," she paused, looking around the room as her brain frantically tried to piece together some semblance of an intelligent argument. In the end she just came back to purity of intent every time.

"I've heard of you. The Sun Wolves – who *hasn't* heard of you? I know, without a doubt, that if you decided to, you could save the abbey – the place I grew up, the place where my only family I've ever known remain. I cannot say that some tragedy kept them from running like everyone else around here. Or at least, not unless you count a system of belief to be a tragedy, and maybe you do. But I *can* tell you that the Daughters are innocents. They don't deserve to be slaughtered by the Aarn, defenseless."

Elya felt her confidence building as she went on, the focus of her plea helping to push past every misgiving or bit of awkwardness that would have otherwise waylaid her. She felt the warmth in her chest begin to heat up, her nerves sending chills of fire down her spine.

"Please, help me. Help them. I know you have loved ones of your own, whoever they might be. I know you understand what it's like to love your home, wherever or whatever your home might be. So please."

By this point, the heat inside of her felt like a raging fire, as Ballian's strength filled her. She spoke out of desire to protect the home, the very thing he most represented. Of course she would have his support.

"Please, help me to protect mine," Elya finished, and then just like that the heat whiffed out, pulling back into her Holy Core while she was left panting, shaking with the remnants of the deific empowerment. No one spoke as they looked at her, stared at her. Elya had no idea what their reaction would be, but she had given it her all. That was all she could do.

"Hm," a deep voice rumbled into the quiet. Elya turned. She could tell who it was right away even with only a single interaction with him. Morgan Arn Rohadi stepped up next to his wife, looking straight at Elya before continuing. "That was dramatic."

Elaine chuckled and it broke the tension, while the Paladin placed a hand on his shoulder.

"Maven is often the naysayer here, and it's good that he can be our voice of reason. The rest of us don't really need to be convinced, however. We're the Sun Wolves. You said it yourself, Elya; you've heard of us. We have a reputation," Morgan continued, his head slowly turning as he met the eyes of warrior present. Asani gave Elya an encouraging nod as she noticed her, standing near the front.

"We aren't about to let that reputation be tarnished by leaving innocents to be killed when we're perfectly capable of stepping in. Are we?" Morgan asked this last thing to the room at large and he was met by a great shout from every throat present.

"No, sir!"

Morgan grinned.

"Then let's go save some idiots!" the Dread Wolf roared, and his pack joined him.

CHAPTER FIVE

Elya's success caught her off guard.

It was an odd thing, that. It felt like such a momentous decision, so of course the push to achieve what she decided to try and do should be just as momentous and challenging. Now, it almost felt like there was no reason for her to have gotten so worked up.

Yet perhaps Ballian had allowed it simply for Elya's benefit. She lifted a silent prayer of thanks to her god as the clamor of movement and the teardown of the Sun Wolves' encampment continued. It had not taken long for their meeting in the command center to conclude, and things had begun to move at a very rapid pace.

Elya now stood with the Fangs, having shouldered the new camping gear she had not even had the chance to use yet and assisting as she was able to with the others.

"To think that my dearest could sway even the cold heart of our precocious Commander Rohadi! Your wonders never cease, darling," Dorian said, startling Elya as he spoke from right next to her. She laughed nervously, mentally scolding herself for growing so wrapped up in her own head.

"I'm sort of confused about it myself," she replied, sifting through the ranger's flowery dramatics to address his actual comment. She was surprised how quickly she was getting used to his antics.

"I'm not," Fahra interjected, having just finished putting her own pack together and slipped it over her shoulders, her weapon now strapped to its side. She approached the two of them as the others were wrapping up. "Something about you just screamed 'leader' from the moment we met."

Elya blushed at the compliment, then glanced over at Harn and Ornn as they got into a lighthearted argument with Riley over their harassment of the ever-gullible Lucem.

"This... is nice. Being a part of all this, I mean. It's barely been any time at all since I got here and I already feel like I fit. When this is done, I don't know how I'm going to be able to just pick up and move on," Elya sighed. Dorian and Fahra exchanged glances, opening their mouths as if they both had something to say, but someone else beat them to the punch.

"Then don't leave. Stay with us. The Fangs could always use another member, and you certainly have the capability to be a great fighter. Combined with your power as a Font, you would make a formidable member of the Sun Wolves."

Elya turned around to find Asani standing there, still in that same armor, a hand on the hilt of her curved sword with her pack on the ground next to her.

"What? Me? Join the Wolves?" she repeated, startled. What was the Captain talking about? There was no way that she was being serious... was there? Was this an actual offer?

"Yes, you," Fahra answered, a huge grin plastered on her face. "I don't think I've ever liked the idea of someone new joining us so much. It's like you were meant to be here, El."

By this point, the twins had heard, as had Lucem and even Riley, who stood nearby with arms crossed as she looked down on their gathering with a smug smile on her face.

"Knew it," the giant woman remarked.

"El! Please!" Lucem said excitedly, his eyes sparkling with joy.

"We approve," the twins said in unison.

Emotion surged as she took in these people she had known for barely two days who now sought to welcome her among them permanently. She felt tears springing to her eyes and blinked them away as quickly as possible.

"I'll just have to discuss it with the Commanders, but I highly doubt there would be any issues with extending you an official invitation," Asani continued. Elya turned and looked at her, thoughts racing.

There was no guarantee she would survive what came next. She knew that, no matter how confident she was in the company. Even if everything turned out perfectly, she also knew that she would never be welcomed back among the Daughters. It was a hard truth, but truth it still was. So was this really her path forward? Had Ballian led her straight into the waiting arms of her own destiny?

"Okay," she said, the word a rasp barely audible until she cleared her throat and met Asani's eyes with resolve.

"Okay!" she said again, this time louder, with a firmness that could not be denied. The Fangs – other than Riley, who instead thumped her chest with her fist and nodded – erupted in cheers. Dorian got down on one knee as if he were going to propose, only to get bowled over by the rest of the squad as they shoved forward to welcome her.

"Let's not get too ahead of ourselves," the Captain laughed, though it was obvious it was not too serious of a correction. "Nothing is official until I speak with

Commanders Lustra and Rohadi. But... yes, Elya. Welcome."

After a round of cheerful, individual congratulations, the group finished packing up their things and carried their supply crates back to where Garth was overseeing a load up of the entirety of the camp's supplies into five wagons that had been rolled up into a semicircle. Horses, presumably used for hauling those wagons, were grazing a short distance away, harnesses on so they could be attached as soon as the loading was completed.

"C'mon, get yerselves in gear! We've a bunch of pious types to be savin' and not the most time to be doin' it, so MOVE!" the Half-Giant was shouting. The Fangs kicked up their own speed, their not-yet-but-maybe-soon new member keeping up since she did not have to haul one of those crates herself.

Asani, Fahra, Lucem and the twins all dropped off their crates on one of the wagons, while Riley followed up with two of them stacked together with barely a hint she was carrying a significantly larger load. Dorian, little weasel that he was, had wandered over just after the last crate had been picked up and so had not needed to assist in the carrying. Instead, he had talked Elya's ear off the whole walk over, discussing all of the wondrous things their merry band of 'gallant warriors' would do with her at their side.

It was endearing, in a very Dorian sort of way. His excitement was palpable. It kept the energy of the squad up, even if it was just because they were going back and forth between chuckling and telling him to be quiet.

Once they were finished loading their crates onto the wagon, they made their way in the same direction as everyone else who had already dropped off their supplies. Squads were lining at the far end of the clearing, in the direction that Elya believed that the abbey lay. Now that this venture was so close to setting out, she could feel her nerves returning. She had never been part of something like this and had barely learned to wield a sword. Sure, she had her abilities as a Font to rely on, but even that was still in the beginning stages of development.

Once they reached the gathering, they could hear Elaine calling out orders.

"We're going to be spreading our individual squads out as we make our way toward Talwich Abbey! Our maps gave us the location of the structure, so we have a clear approximation of our arrival time. We'll be calling squads up one at a time and giving your Captains individual orders, so listen closely!" the Paladin shouted.

Tension was still high, as it had been that morning when Elya and Elaine had returned to camp from their nighttime training, but now that tension had been given direction. An outlet.

Everyone was eager to get moving and meet the threat to come with all the strength that had made the Sun Wolves so renowned.

There were plenty of reasons Elya could be nervous, but still... seeing all of this, she could not help but be curious as to what would come.

"Elya," someone said, the voice appearing very suddenly from behind the Fangs. Even Asani whirled to see who it was. Maven stood there, the Wizard looking as intimidating as ever.

"Maven," she answered him, looking to the rest of the Fangs to see if she was the only one thrown off by his sudden appearance. The abject horror on Lucem's face made her smile, at least. "Do you need me?" she asked.

"Commander Lustra has given instruction that you are to travel with her today while the Fangs survey their assigned grid and has sent me to collect you. Is that the proper use for a Wizard's talents? I would not think so. However, I am not in charge here, so I digress," Maven continued, his sudden descent into complaint confusing Elya for a moment. It was not a long moment, but it still seemed enough to perturb the Wizard as his brow scrunched up.

"Well, are you coming with me?" he asked. Shaking her head to clear the weirdness of the moment, Elya looked at Asani who nodded.

"Go on, El. I'll make sure to speak with the Commanders tonight about what we all discussed. I promise," Asani told her. That said, Elya looked back to Maven.

"Lead on," she told him. With a snort, the man turned and started walking right that moment, forcing Elya to say a quick goodbye to the others and hurry after him. The Wizard took her on a long, loping route along the outside edge of the gathering until Elaine and Morgan came into view.

"Ah! Elya, good, you're here," the Paladin exclaimed, once they saw her approach. "Thank you, Maven. That done, see what you can of the Horde today - if there are visible traces of their coming in any direction, if there's any sign of the other creature, anything."

Maven bowed.

"Of course, Commander. Gladly."

Just like that the Wizard was gone, leaving Elya to stand awkwardly next to Elaine and Morgan, who had locked his eyes onto her the moment she came into view.

"I knew you would have something interesting to ask," said the Paladin through a chuckle, before turning back to the waiting squads and stepping away to continue the task of assigning duties.

"You!" she called, pointing at a nearby group. "Front and center, let's go!"

As Elaine went, leaving Elya to stand with Morgan, she started to wonder if now would be a good time to ask about the odd behavior he and a few others had exhibited toward her since the night of her arrival. It was a mystery that felt like a weight in her stomach, following her everywhere she went. Then Morgan spoke and the opportunity was lost to her.

"You're brave, you know."

The comment took her off guard. She looked at Morgan, and her face must have betrayed her confusion because it prompted him to continue.

"You stood up for the people you care about and got thrown out of your home for it. That was brave on its own, and most 'brave' folk that I've met in my life would have left it at that and run for the hills. But you?" Morgan paused here, scoffing as he shook his head. "You take the first chance you get to try and help them. You go in front of a group with our reputation – and by the Pantheon, we have a reputation, for good or for ill – and you actually have the gall to ask for help, even though you have nothing to give in return. You're brave."

It was the most Elya had heard the man speak in a single conversation, and she found herself completely absorbed in his words. Something about the man just drew her in, some strange otherworldliness that she did not understand. All of the Sun Wolves had earned their place in the guild, she knew that. All of them were skilled, and the greatest of them were the subject of stories you normally would only hear of the Heroic Age. Yet Morgan?

Morgan Arn Rohadi was the Dread Wolf. The Midnight Sun. People said he slew the Azyrian Demon single-handedly. That the Sultans of the Dunelands far to the West whispered of the failed Scouring, where their armies were crushed when they came up against the militias of the Central Kingdoms with him at their lead. That even the Last Dragon had come against his might and turned tail, fleeing for its life.

Even within the Sun Wolves, the man was mythical.

She knew that many of the stories were likely exaggerated far beyond their initial scope. She knew that before her now was just a man, no matter who he was. Yet still.

Still, something about his myth pulled her in as he spoke, held her attention as though every word from his mouth was the most important thing she could ever hear from mortal man. Which was why she was filled with a flood of pride as he spoke of her bravery… and why what he said next sucked that pride right back out of her.

"I have found that bravery is the most valued ideal of the dead, Elya."

The words made her flinch. She could take a blow. She could call on that place inside of her, that strength that had kept her going most of her life even if it was the kind of strength looked down upon by Mother Moira. Even when she had been thrown from her place in the Order, she had stood tall.

For all of that, his words made her shrink back like no other wound she had ever suffered. Tears sprang to her eyes, unbidden and unwelcome. His words should not hurt her so, so why? Why did they?

"Let others be brave now. Set it aside. You've done what you hoped you would do. We will save the abbey and the Daughters of Ballian. You will be free to live whatever life you wish to when we are done here. So, for the love of every god and goddess that sits upon the Pantheonic Thrones, let this task be the last you need call on bravery for. Set death and danger aside and live the sort of life you are meant to: one of peace, and quiet, far away from the horrors of the world," Morgan continued, standing straight and bringing his hands together behind his back as he spoke. His eyes were hard, boring into her like claws and ripping her open.

Thoughts of a future with the Fangs, a new place to call her own, among people she could truly be friends with, disappeared. Cold, hard reality struck her full in the face. If this was how Morgan felt, he would never grant Elya permission to join the Sun Wolves.

It would not matter how Asani made the suggestion. If the Dread Wolf did not want someone to join, then there was nothing anyone could do about it.

Seeing the tears springing to Elya's eyes, Morgan left it. He crossed his arms and looked away, toward where his wife was hard at work organizing their guild members, leaving the young Font to her thoughts. And there she stayed, until a short while later Elaine walked over, nodding to Morgan.

"Alright then. It's time to go. Elya, are you ready?" she asked, turning to look at her as she spoke before she noticed the pallor that had fallen over her.

"Are you alright?" Elaine continued, turning to fully face the younger woman now. But Elya only shook her head.

"I'll be fine. We have somewhere to be, right?" she said quietly. Morgan grunted and nodded.

"She's not wrong. Let's go," he said, before turning and walking into the trees. Elya followed a moment later, leaving Elaine to stare after them before her brows twisted in anger.

"You old fool, what did you say to her?" she called after him, though she was ignored. The wagons were already trundling along, however, Garth and a select few chosen to attend to them and the horses simply following Morgan's lead.

"Morgan Arn Rohadi, by the blood of the Pantheon, we're going to have words," she muttered. Then she was moving too. After all, they had somewhere to be. Words would have to wait.

Elya walked for the hours that followed in a muted state. It was like the world around her had lost its luster, her joy at a newfound future replaced by the loss she had warned Fahra she wanted to avoid.

She was a fool for ever thinking such a life could be hers.

Nothing stirred her from her numb march through the forest, eyes fixed on Morgan's back, until – as the sun was nearing the end of its journey across the sky – they left the tree line once again for a vast meadow that Elya knew intimately. A field of multi-colored flowers, with a large pond at one end, where on days their workload had been lighter, she and some of the girls had gone fishing when the weather permitted.

At the other end of the meadow lay Talwich Abbey, its ancient construction and soaring belltower as beautiful as she remembered it. Vines crept up along its cracked outer walls, which surrounded it as a small breaker against outside threats. Elya knew that once, when it had first been constructed, the Pantheonic Templars protected all such holy sites in Eran. It would have had a permanent, if small, garrison of troops that ensured the safety of those who lived there.

Now, she knew that the path that ran along the top of that wall was mostly used to dry laundry and grow crops.

The huge gate at the front and center of the abbey walls opened directly into the structure, a design choice that Elya had never really considered much until now, after having spent some time around warriors. It was those gates she had walked through after her confrontation with Mother Moira in the chapel. Once she had wondered what adventures might await her in the greater world beyond the abbey as she looked out from inside.

"Ballian give me strength," she whispered, her connection with her deity the only thing she felt firm enough to lean on now. It would be all she had once the abbey had been saved, after all.

"Syranna will be with us as well, Elya. I feel her will in this."

Elaine's words, spoken from next to her where she had frozen upon setting eyes on her former home, startled Elya from her reverie. She looked over at the Paladin, trying to grasp what she meant before she realized the woman had to have thought she was asking for Ballian's strength to face the danger ahead, not the personal struggle that roiled within.

"Thank you, Elaine. I believe she will be, as well. And… thank you. For taking the time to teach me, even if it was only a single night. It means more than you could know," Elya replied, forcing a small smile on her face for the sake of the woman's kindness.

Something in the way she spoke must have been off because Elaine turned to face her, placing a hand on the head of her hammer, one finger tapping on it in a steady pattern.

"By the Abyss, El! What did my idiot of a husband say to you?!" she demanded. Elya paused, considering. Should she say? They had not known one another long, but Elya felt she understood the Paladin well enough to know that she would be furious with Morgan for the way he spoke to her, even if she possibly agreed with what he had said. Did she really want to cause an argument between the two of them?

No. No, she did not.

"Nothing bad. Just… the truth," she answered, giving a retracted version of what had happened. She felt tears trying to work their way out of her eyes again and hid it by pretending to clear her throat, rubbing them away before Elaine noticed.

"The truth? The... Elya, I want to make sure I'm understanding correctly. He told you the truth? As in, the *truth,* truth?" the woman demanded, startling her with the tone she took. What? Why was that what she was getting caught up in? What else could truth possibly...

Her eyes widened, mind going back over all the moments she had noticed the strangeness among the leaders of the Sun Wolves regarding her name and her identity. How only the oldest members of the guild reacted in that way. Elya locked eyes with Elaine.

"What truth do *you* think he told me?" she asked, quietly. Searching the woman's face. Hoping she would say it, that she would explain whatever it was that had been bugging her so badly since she had first realized something was being kept from her.

Elaine knew she had messed up. Elya saw it on her face, even if the Paladin was able to quickly school her expression into passivity. But it was enough.

"Nothing, Elya. I'll... I'll speak with my husband about it," she replied.

It was enough to know Elaine knew the truth and had just lied to her.

Another piece of her connection to the Wolves froze over and fall apart in that moment as she shrank away from Elaine. The bond she had begun to feel with the Paladin withered to almost nothing.

"I see," Elya said, woodenly, as though every word had to be forced. "Go on, then. Speak with him."

Elaine stared into her face as wagons passed. They would gather in the middle of the meadow until a defensive plan had been decided on, Elya knew. Right now she did not care. Right now, she stared straight back at the other Font with a coldness she didn't know she possessed. So much so that she felt just the smallest bit of the warmth in her chest, in her Holy Core, leech away.

"Elya, I-" Elaine began, but Elya snapped before another word left her lips.

"Just go. Leave me be."

Elaine waited long enough for it to be noticeable, not breaking their eye contact… until finally she sighed and closed her eyes.

"Alright, El. I'll leave you alone. Just… stay in sight. Okay?"

Elya did not answer, turning her head to look away. A moment later she could hear the Paladin's armored boots as she left. She was not sure how long she stayed there, watching while the group she had arrived with started removing supply crates from one of the wagons while a party of three split off to make their way toward the abbey itself. If she looked closely, she could make out a few people already up on the walls looking out at where the Wolves were gathered. They were probably wondering if they were about to be robbed on the eve of the Aarn attack, considering they would have no idea why else warriors would be setting up just outside.

Elya closed her eyes, taking a deep breath as she tried to center herself.

"Ballian, strengthen me to face the things I cannot on my own," she breathed. Her Holy Core surged, its heat restored as she felt the mental touch of a brief connection with her god. The heat poured out of her chest and filled her body, burning away the numbness that had settled within.

She was not okay. She had no idea what her future would be when this was all said and done. But for now, she could set all of that aside to focus on the immediate task:

Keeping Talwich Abbey and its inhabitants alive.

Elya set off across the field after the group already halfway to the abbey's gates, determined to do what she could to make things go as smoothly as possible... as long as her presence did not make things worse, instead.

"Ah! El, yer here!" Garth proclaimed as Elya approached, the party of Sun Wolves having stopped before the gates where they waited for someone to come and speak with them. "I was wonderin' where ya ran off to."

The Half-Giant grinned as he spoke, planting one of his enormous hands on her head. Despite her interactions with the Commanders, she could not help the smile that spread on her face at the man's warm greeting. She liked the friendly giant. Something about him just seemed safe to her. Still, she was not sure how to respond, her gaze turning to take in Maven – who had at some point returned and was indifferent to her presence – and Elaine, who kept glancing back at her with a sort of urgent awkwardness.

"I just needed some time to think, that's all," she finally said, returning Garth's smile with one of her own just in time for the abbey's gates to begin creaking open. The full gates, and not just the smaller door set into them. Inside, they could see several of the Daughters working together to open the heavy things, straining so much their faces were turning red.

"Let me help y'all with that!" Garth cried, hurrying forward. He put his shoulder to one door and with his inhuman strength, shoved. It practically flew the rest of the way open, the women who had been pushing on it almost flying backwards. He quickly helped with the other side and then stepped back, affording Elya a look at the garden she had walked through on her way out and the old crone who stood waiting there, head held high in her habit as she took in the arrivals with a sneer.

"And what brings a band of unfaithful heathens to our doors on the eve of divine punishment? I will tell you now, we shelter only those who call Ballian their Lord, or one of his kin," Moira rasped, her fierce gaze piercing the front of their group as though they were nothing but a bother. If it mattered to any of them, Elya could not see it.

"We won't be needing shelter, ma'am," Elaine began, stepping forward before pressing an arm across her chest, fist clenched, and bowed. "My name is Elaine de Lustra, and I am a Paladin of Syranna. With me are Garth Damassi, the Half-Giant, and Maven, Wizard of the Circle. We are members of the company known as the Sun Wolves and are here in answer to a request to protect you and your abbey from the Horde."

Whispers erupted from the assembled Daughters immediately. Elya was not the only one who had heard the stories, after all. Even Moira seemed surprised, her eyes widening just a touch. Not much, but enough for someone who had spent more than two decades under her purview to notice. Elya smiled.

It was like her smile was a beacon. The Mother of Talwich Abbey turned, locking onto the change in her expression with narrowed eyes.

"You introduced three of the four of you present, Lady Lustra, but neglected to offer the name of... your..." Moira trailed off as she looked, *really* looked, at Elya. Saw the details of her face. Then she recoiled, rage clouding her features as she turned back toward Elaine, automatic religious instinct making her avert her eyes.

"Lady Lustra, I appreciate a servant of the Great Ballian's sister coming to render protection to us in this time, but are you aware you have with you an individual who has been excommunicated from the Order of Ballian and has subsequently been banned from all holy sites related to our Lord?!" she snarled. A wild change came to her face, wrinkles twisting with true anger.

Daughters – women who Elya knew as family – were once more reacting, this time out of some mix of shock or horror or anger or... she honestly did not know what. But they all saw her as she took a step forward, out from behind Garth so she was not hidden in the slightest. She tilted her head up, eyes scanning everyone in the gateway and beyond as they all tried to look anywhere but at her.

"Apologies, ma'am, but the only individual with us who is a faithful of Ballian is Elya here – a woman I happen to know from personal confirmation is a Font of your Lord, and as such is proven to have his favor," Elaine replied smoothly, not even batting a lash at the Mother's rage.

The instant confusion on Moira's face, followed by slowly dawning horror, made Elya grin despite everything in her saying she should not feel so good about this.

"That- that can't... what are you talking about? Has she tricked you somehow?" the old woman asked, the aggression in her tone suddenly cooled.

"I've done nothing of the sort," Elya interjected, taking another step forward so that she was beside Elaine. Maybe it was the dramatic turn of events over the last twenty-four hours – though this week had been dramatic in its entirety, so narrowing it to a single day's time of events leading to this might have been a bit limiting – but she felt a surge of aggressive pride then, knowing that the Mother's arrogant belief that she knew better than their Lord was being upended this very moment.

A vein in Moira's neck bulged as her face turned red. It was likely taking everything she had not to turn and snap at Elya directly, but to do that she would have to break her own precious beliefs. It would be admitting defeat, which she could never allow herself to do.

"As she said," Elaine said, throwing a look her way as she purposely rubbed Moira's nose in it, "there is no deception here. I witnessed Ballian's power flowing through her myself. It was one of the strongest showings of holy investiture I have ever witnessed, and I have met several other Fonts in my lifetime."

Even when Elya had left, when she had noted Moira's fear of her and what it could mean, the woman had not been at a loss for words. She had still done what she could to turn the situation to her favor, as she had always seemed capable of doing. Yet here, for the first time that she could remember, Mother Moira was at a loss for words.

"But… I…" she stuttered, eyes darting between the Paladin's face as though desperate to see deception there and Elya's general direction, still refusing to look *at* her.

"If we can come inside and discuss things with you, I'm sure that we can alleviate your confusion. Then we can move on and talk about the most important thing; namely, the safety of you and everyone else living in your abbey. Does that seem fair?" Elaine continued, smiling a sweet smile that did not reach her eyes.

Still Moira was reeling, shaken by this turn of events. After several long, tense moments she finally narrowed her eyes and grit her teeth.

"I'm afraid the lot of you are not welcome within our walls. Begone with you, now!" the Mother snapped. From the looks the Daughters were giving one another around her, though, they did not seem to appreciate this. "Shut the gates!" the crone continued, hissing the command at the girls who had opened them.

Garth took a step forward, into the gateway, and stood at attention. Elaine shook her head and walked inside, stopping just to the side of Moira and placing a hand on her shoulder.

"I'm afraid I insist," the Paladin said simply. Maven followed her in, the arcane tattoos on his body drawing the focus of most of the girls while Garth turned and looked to Elya.

"Comin' in, El?" he asked.

"NO!" Moira shouted, her body heaving and shaking as she tried to step around Elaine, as though she would physically stop this from happening. "I don't care what lies you spout, that Abyssal whore may not set foot inside-"

Ballian's presence descended.

Elya felt it as a palpable force, a rage that his chosen, his Font, would ever be declared something so vile as a servant of the Abyss. That someone who purported to worship him had said it?! Heat surged in her chest, filling her the quickest it ever had as a holy anger twisted her features. Light erupted from her eyes, her nose, her mouth – anywhere it could leave her body, it did.

"Ballian didn't like that," Elya said, eyes narrowing. "He didn't like that one bit."

Moira could not take this. Could not take the proof right before her eyes. She clenched at her chest, horror and pain flashing across her face before she collapsed. Elya, shocked, took a step back, the light ebbing somewhat while everyone else save Maven stared.

The Wizard stepped over to the old woman's prone form, checking for a pulse. He looked up, eyes finding Elaine before he spoke, as evenly as always.

"She's dead."

CHAPTER SIX

It was quiet in the chapel as Elya stood up on the small, raised pulpit at its front.

Ahead of her stood Elaine, the Paladin at rest with her hands clasped in front of her as she addressed the gathered Daughters of Ballian. On the other side of Elaine stood Moira's replacement, the next most senior member of the Order present at Talwich Abbey after the late Mother. Dianne Telora was a Daughter Elect, one who chose to join the Order of her own volition. While a good fifteen years younger than Moira, she was still in her late sixties. Elya knew her well, of course, as all the others.

Dianne was the quiet, subservient sort who until now had been quite content letting someone else dictate their life to them. For her to now be the religious head of Talwich Abbey was… well. There could be worse. But there could be significantly better, too. The Order would likely send someone official to either confirm her appointment or relieve her of duty and assign someone new to take things over. Elya was praying they would assign someone, for the everyone's sake.

"It is, in short, a simple thing," Elaine was saying, the very picture of a holy warrior. "So long as you all remain within your walls and barricade your gates, the Aarn will not bother with trying to break in. Especially not with our defense outside. Their goal lies in the North, and everything they destroy along the way is ultimately just collateral."

The whole chapel was silent as they listened. Elya could see Garth, humongous man that he was, standing at the far end of the single aisle that ran down the center of the pews, keeping an eye on the hall outside. Maven had posted himself up on the wall, performing spellcraft of some kind to once again ascertain how far the Horde was.

With its arrival so close, it felt as though every moment grew heavier.

"If that's the case, then wasn't Mother Moira right in the end? We would have been fine if we just stayed put," someone in the pews asked. Dianne – was it Mother Dianne now? – locked her gaze on the speaker immediately, face turning red.

"Josephine! Watch your tone!" Dianne cried, a shrill noise that hurt Elya's head. Then she turned toward Elaine. "My apologies, Lady Paladin!"

The Sun Wolf Commander smiled and shook her head.

"No worries, Dianne. It's an understandable question to ask, truly," she replied, soothing the panic of the interim Mother before addressing the Daughter, Josephine, as well. "In truth, young lady, the largest reason for your safety in this will be our presence outside. The Aarn are a tribal folk, and take challenge in stride. If we prove a fierce enough bulwark for them to break themselves against, since we do not possess what they are after, they will eventually turn aside and let us be. It will be a strain to prove ourselves to be a fierce enough threat, but the important part is that we *will*. So long as they are not provoked by the sight of... well, let's just say they consider noncombatants an offense."

This elicited a round of quiet exclamations and conversation across the chapel as the women took in this new information. Elya cocked her head to the side, looking at Elaine. How had she not ever thought to ask her or any of the other Sun Wolves if they had seen the Aarn before? With all their experience, it was no surprise that they had.

"Now, if that's everything, my friends and I have work to do. There's only one other thing that we must do here. Elya, could you come forward please?"

The request startled her.

'What?'

She had thought that the Paladin wanted her here so that the Daughters would have someone they know in front of them as this information was delivered. Someone they could trust was being truthful, even if they could not look at her because of her status in the Order. What was she up to?

Realizing that she had not moved yet and Elaine was still staring at her expectantly, Elya jolted into action, taking the steps that brought her up just next to the silver-haired woman. She, in turn, spun to face Dianne.

"Dianne, if you could come here as well?" she asked, and the interim Mother jumped before hurriedly moving over as well, though she was very awkwardly trying not to look at Elya as she did so.

Once they were both next to her, Elaine looked out on the filled chapel once more, bringing her hands together in a clap that eerily reminded Elya of when Moira had struck her in this same place.

"Several of you saw for yourselves already, but for those who were not there when we arrived at the front gates, I have something to say. Elya, this young woman beside me who you have all known since she was brought here as a young girl, was excommunicated from your Order just days ago. Right here, in front of all you, if I'm not mistaken. However, I'm telling you today that this was a mistake," she began. Of course, Elya was alarmed immediately, as was Dianne and what looked like almost every other Daughter in the room. Elaine just kept going.

"Your now tragically passed Mother, Moira, witnessed this day Elya's holy power granted to her as a Font of Ballian," she continued, yet could get no further before outcry erupted in the room. Shouts of disbelief and anger flew at them, drowning out anything else she was going to say. After her patience was exhausted, Elaine finally turned to look at Elya. Only a few of the women in the room were not reacting this way, the ones who had been there when Moira died, and they were staring white-faced at their companions. It was obvious that a demonstration was needed for things to continue the way the Paladin had planned.

Sighing, Elya drew on her Holy Core once more. Ballian's light erupted from her, bringing the room a wonderful, glorious warmth that also silenced the clamor. Into that stillness, Elaine spoke.

"Is that proof enough for you all?" She said it with a grin, and Elya took a deep breath in as though it would help her to hold this moment forever in her mind. Then she released the power with a sigh, letting the light in the room return to normal. It was beginning to grow tedious, constantly drawing on her Holy Core to do nothing but glow.

"Now that we've established that the Lord Ballian has personally shown his favor for her, it makes things simple. Dianne, I believe it is in the vested interest of your god and your people here that Elya's excommunication be undone, immediately."

Dianne looked out at the room, still dead silent at the display of divine light. She looked at Elaine, the Paladin watching expectantly. Then she looked at Elya, actually looked at her, and sighed.

"We have wronged you, beloved of Ballian," Dianne said, just loud enough for Elya to hear. Then she got a bit louder, so the room was able to listen, though her voice was shaky with nerves. "Let me correct our sin."

Elaine – coming to stand behind Dianne – gave Elya another nod. Elya, grateful for this despite the woman's lies, nodded back. And Dianne placed her hand on the Blessed Scriptures and undid her excommunication.

So why did it all feel so... pointless?

"My Wizard's Sight gives us approximately ten hours before they reach us."

Maven's declaration quieted the group that was assembled at the center of a vast flurry of activity in the area just outside the abbey's gates. All around, Sun Wolves were working to construct quick and dirty defensive positions and fortifications under the shouted directions of Garth. Each time one of the squads that had been sent out returned, they had been assigned new jobs as part of this activity, gradually amping up the scope until only two squads remained absent, one of which were the Fangs.

The longer Asani and the others were gone, the higher Elya's stress built. They were her friends, new though it may have been and in spite of her impending departure from the Wolves' company after... well, after.

Now, to hear just how soon all of this would be coming to a head added yet another thing to what had become a mountain of issues weighing her down.

"And your estimation of their numbers remains the same?" Morgan responded, once again standing at rest with one hand clasping his other behind his back. He had foregone his armor while assisting the myriad construction projects ongoing across the meadow, opting for a form fitting black tunic that left his arms bare and cotton pants of the same color and similar fit. The mild heat had him sweating lightly, but he looked uneffected by the physical work otherwise.

"Yes, Commander. Based off historical examples of an Aarn Horde coming to Eran, there should be somewhere along the line of 10,000 to 12,000 Aarn present in this most recent assault, an educated guess that I believe my visual study of their approach in the last two weeks has confirmed," the Wizard answered, and Morgan nodded.

"Thank you, Maven. Go and perform your duties for our defenses and then get some rest. We need you in perfect condition for the fight ahead of us," he told the man. Maven bowed then turned away, already gathering Mana in his hands. Elya watched for a moment longer than the others, the power at the Wizard's command still a marvel to her. She turned away after seeing him begin to raise ramparts from the ground, the earth shaking beneath their feet from the force controlling it.

Magic. What a power.

By the time she refocused on the conversation, things had already moved on.

"- but it's not impossible, so long as we stick to our plan and our other issue is resolved. No one identified it so far?" Morgan had continued. It took Elya a moment to catch on to what he was talking about, and another moment to be okay with focusing on what the man was saying after the last conversation they had had together. This time, though, it was Morgan, Elaine, and several others that she had not met but who seemed to be company veterans.

"No. Whatever creature has moved into the area as others abandoned it, we have only found signs of its passing. Mutilated animals in the forest, damaged trees, droppings and the like. Unless one of our two remaining squads in the field find something, we're going to have to watch out for that variable once things get violent," Elaine replied, followed by a chorus of affirmations from the others.

"What creature?" Elya interrupted, having coasted through most of this meeting by standing quietly to the side while everyone else spoke. Talk of mutilated animals brought to mind the wolf she literally fell on and its devastated pack before Dorian had found her.

Morgan glanced her way then sighed, rubbing his forehead.

"There's a monster of some sort that has inserted itself into the area with the absence of so many other natural predators. With the Horde on its way, most things should have fled. It makes sense – the Aarn bring with them the fury of the Frozen Wastes across the ocean to the South, their *skaerig* witches capable of commanding the ice and snow and calling it down wherever they go. But something dangerous, something strong enough not to be scared off by that, has been hunting in the woods. We were hoping to get eyes on it and at least confirm that it wouldn't be a threat to any of us before facing the Horde, but so far there's been no luck," he explained. Elya's eyes widened, then, with the realization that she had been wandering alone in the woods with that sort of monster on the loose. She had even stumbled on the remains of some of its prey.

She could have died before even discovering that she was a Font, let alone meeting the Sun Wolves and having her life and dreams change before her eyes.

"Oh," she said aloud, the most eloquent thing her brain could give her to say. Elaine's mouth quirked up a bit.

"'Oh,' indeed," Morgan grumbled. Then he turned back to his warriors, opening his mouth to continue on with what he had prepared to say, only to be interrupted by shouts from the direction of the forest.

"Help! We need help!" someone cried. Elaine bolted immediately, barely a pause between their words and her action.

"Get to your squads, now!" Morgan shouted at his men before turning and starting after his wife. Elya stood there, frozen with horror, because she had recognized that voice.

"Dorian?!" she rasped aloud. Then she, too, was running. There was a commotion at the tree line as someone limped into view, bow drawn and arrow nocked. The figure was alternating between looking up at the sky and glancing behind him, back into the trees. She knew before she got close enough to see the details of their face that it was him. Horror filled her at the realization he was hurt.

She felt her Holy Core reacting to her emotional state, power filling her. There was a roar, a shape slithering just out of view, trees trembling at its passing. Shouts of pain and combat rent the air. Elaine called out, answered by a burst of sound and light like the rising sun. The sun's light grew denser, stronger, coalescing as something real and solid before roiling forth in a wave. It bypassed Dorian, who fell over, landing on his back and firing an arrow at whatever he was running from. The light swept on, until something cried out and all of it suddenly condensed further, a beam striking one, specific area.

There was silence.

Then Morgan was in the trees, a great, obsidian blade called to his hands from nothing. Runes, etched along its length, flared with a burning, dread glow, a green so dark it could not come from any natural thing like the holy might of Syranna or Ballian. Trees trembled and another sound came, a strange, sibilant rumble, low and wholly *wrong*. Elaine was there next, several of those that had been attending their meeting close on her heels. Other warriors poured forth, weapons drawn.

Elya reached the prone Dorian, feeling sick at the sight of his leg, torn open at his thigh and shin, the bone visible as blood poured forth. His veins webbed out, black and wrong, from his wounds.

"H- h- hey, gor... geous..." Dorian rasped on seeing her, trying to smile. Blood of the Pantheon, he tried to smile. He was pale, sweating, his whole body visibly shaking. Elaine fell at his side, thoughts a mess, not able to think anything coherent. The ranger continued, despite his state. "N- no n- need t- t- to... look s- so sad..."

"Ballian, help me... Oh gods, help *him*..." Elya rasped. The heat in her body was becoming uncomfortable, her physical form filled to the brim with holy power.

"I... I'll b- be o... okay. It'll all... be..." Dorian trailed off, body beginning to grow still. She had to act. She had to act now, or he would be dead. He would be dead, and she could not allow that. Would not allow that. She breathed in deep, placed her hands on her friend's leg, and released her breath with a shout as Ballian's power flowed through her.

Elya shouted at the outpouring of sheer holy might.

Heat poured from her, steam beginning to rise from Dorian as it transferred to him. The black veins rapidly receded, bones snapping and righting themselves, his spilled blood evaporating. He heaved a breath as deep as Elya's and his eyes snapped open. He bolted upright with a cry. Tears began to stream down his face and he wiped at them, mouth agape.

"How?! What did you... ?"

Elya wanted to respond, wanted to try and explain, but a great weariness fell on her and she slumped back. She was breathless, vision dimming along the edges in the aftermath of performing the miracle in Ballian's name. She dimly remembered Elaine's warnings about Evocations, about working to grow her limits so that when she used so much holy power at once it did not leave her useless and depleted. Like right now.

She fell back into the grass, head tilting to the side where she saw a massive, winged serpent with humanoid arms flailing into view, fighting the Sun Wolves, trees beginning to collapse in the chaos.

A flash of green light, followed by an actual, lupine howl, and she watched the massive monster's head fall from its body.

Then Dorian was there, their positions reversed as he panicked.

"El?! Elya, are you okay?! What's wrong?!" he was shouting, but his words sounded distant, like he was far away from her.

Darkness came, then, and Elya knew nothing at all.

The next time that Elya knew anything again, it was a throbbing headache. It pulsed in time with her heartbeat, each wave of pain sending shocks of excruciating pain through her system. She gasped, the noise drawing someone's attention.

"Elya?! Are you awake?!" that someone asked. The voice was familiar, but the noise lanced her brain with more pain and she could not recognize who it was. She turned and vomited, the pressure on her head alleviating somewhat once she was finished.

"Go get the Commander!" the voice continued, the sound of someone running away following a moment later. Then the person crouched at her side. She heard whoever it was – someone male, she noted through the fog over her thoughts – doing something with water, and then there was a repeated dragging sound. Were they cleaning up her sick?

Groaning, Elya tried to open her eyes, but the light forced them shut again almost immediately. It made her gasp, a jolt of fresh pain stabbing into her skull.

"Just rest. It's okay," the person beside her said, keeping his voice low and soothing, as though he had realized from her reaction that speaking too loudly was not a good idea.

She groaned, meaning to thank him but unable to get discernible words out. The person chuckled lightly.

"You're welcome," he said, guessing her intention.

Elya was not sure how much time passed before the dragging sound stopped, but it was followed by something plopping into water and a sigh.

"Who... ?" she finally managed to say, the pain in her head calming just enough for a single word to leave her lips.

"It's Luce, El," he replied, and finally her brain made the connection. Lucem. Luce, the youngest of the Fangs. Even through her exhaustion and pain, she managed to smile, cracking her eyes just enough to see his silhouette, limned in dull moonlight. He was okay. She was so glad he was okay. But...

"The others..." Elya rasped, trying to force out a full question and failing.

"Don't worry about that right now," Luce urged her, his hand grasping hers gently and giving it a light squeeze before pulling away.

She wanted to tell him that worrying was all she could do, wanted to ask him to please, tell her what happened, but the sound of multiple hurried people approaching turned her attention from his vague form to the entrance of the tent. She caught sight of the verdant moon before someone blocked her view and the flap of the tent was pulled back.

"Elya!" someone cried, falling at her other side and immediately, fitfully checking her over. This voice she knew, too, the last she had heard before passing out, though his volume made her wince. The fresh pain almost undid what little recovery her mind had managed.

"Dorian... ?" she gasped, just a bit stronger than before, her vision clearer. The ranger nodded frantically.

"Yes, yes! It's me. Praise the Pantheon, you're awake," Dorian answered, still too loud, before Luce shushed him.

Realizing his error, the ranger quickly lowered his voice. "Sorry, El. Gods, I'm glad you're okay."

"Gods, indeed," a third person said, this voice feminine but commanding and, indeed, familiar. Elya turned to look up at Elaine as she entered the tent. The small space had already been crowded, and now felt egregiously cramped. Ballian's crown, though, she was glad to see them.

"What... happened?" she asked, and the Commander paused before looking at the others.

"Wait outside. At a distance, mind you. We need some privacy," Elaine told them. Luce nodded his understanding, smiling at Elya before getting to his feet and shuffling carefully around the Paladin and out of the tent. Dorian was far more reluctant to go, having just arrived, but with a pointed glare from his superior he finally stood.

"Fine," he hissed, then exited the tent as well – noticeably, with not even a hint of a limp.

Elaine waited until their footsteps faded before letting herself collapse to the ground, no longer hiding her exhaustion. She looked... Syranna help her, she looked her age. Her silver hair stuck out as nearer to gray as she rubbed at her eyes, a tired smile lighting her lips.

"What a disaster," the woman said. Elya tensed, not liking that choice of words in the slightest.

"Please tell me they're alive. Please," she almost begged. Tears pricked at her eyes despite her tiredness. Elaine grimaced, leaning her head back.

"The Fangs are all alive, though not in the best condition. I was able to stabilize them, but for me to heal them entirely would have overtaxed my Core on the eve of the Horde's arrival. Asani sustained only the most minor of injuries, and Lucem miraculously made it out without a scratch, but the others... Blood of the Pantheon, we never thought that an Abyssal *visper* would be here," the woman said. Hearing that her friends were all alive, even if they were not whole, helped to settle her enough to process the rest of what Elaine was saying.

"What... is a visper?" Elya asked, collecting herself enough to push through the fog entirely. She wanted... no, she needed to be fully present for this. She needed to fully comprehend what had happened.

Elaine spat her answer like it was poison.

"A visper is an incredibly rare, serpent-like monster that's known to travel between places charged with death, potential or realized, to hunt and prey on the fearful or weak. Its presence explains all the slaughtered animals we have found in the forest since we got here. Like the wolf corpses you found, before Dorian found you. It kills to inflict pain and terror, then feeds on the negative emotions of the slain. It's a beast straight from the upper layers of the Abyss and should not have been here."

The Paladin paused and took a steadying breath, which was good for Elya considering that her mind was whirling at the thought that this had been a true creature of the Under Realm. She may not have heard of a visper, but she knew that anything born of that demonic place was a horror that had to be destroyed.

"Now..." Elaine said, picking back up with her explanation after calming down. "Nearly an entire squad is dead, with only two survivors, and they're only alive because the Fangs found them and joined the fight before they were completely wiped out – only to then sustain terrible injuries themselves. Riley was..."

The Paladin paused, swallowed, cleared her throat.

"Riley was crushed, most of the bones in her body pulverized. I spent the majority of my time with her, undoing the worst of the damage so she could live long enough for me to recover and finish her healing... as long as we make it past the assault of the Aarn. Fahra had a broken arm and was bitten. The venom ravaged her body before I could stop it, and it will be a while before she's back in fighting condition. The twins... Harn managed to make it out with a bite and lacerations to his chest and stomach from the creature's claws, but Ornn... he lost an arm."

There was silence. Elya stared, body rigid as the tears started to flow. Despite her weakness, despite the fact that it sent more waves of agony down her neck into her back, she sat up, meeting Elaine's eyes straight on.

"I'm being honest now, El. I know that I lied to you before. There are things... things that Morgan and I cannot share because we do not want to influence whatever decision you make for your future," the woman continued, gesturing vaguely into the air before clenching her fists.

"We were taken by surprise here, and lives were lost. More lives will likely be lost as we face the Horde, no matter how confident we are of succeeding. That is the reality of our life. This is what it is to be one of us, to kill for a living. We risk our lives every single time we take a job. Maybe you think we're heroic. Maybe you think our actions to be noble. That doesn't change the reality we face in taking those actions. Death is a constant companion to us, Elya. We know it intimately, and it knows us. Asani spoke to me, and I spoke to Morgan. I know what was said to you, both by the Fangs and by my husband. So please, whatever decision you make for yourself, hear me. Hear this."

Elya was quiet, could only nod. Even her tears had stopped.

"There are many lives we can lead. We are all of us the sum of our choices, the decisions we make as we face crossroads in our lives. Sometimes, those choices lead us to things that are good, and right, and worthwhile. Other times, the things we do and the actions we take damn us, the same as any demon or other being of the Under Realm might. You have to decide for yourself what kind of life you want to live. If you see what we are, if you know what we do and what we have to live with every single day, can you truly choose to be one of us and carry the consequences of that decision forever? Because once you're in, no matter how hard you try, you'll never really leave this life. It will follow you forever. And forever can be a very, very long time."

Elaine stood, her expression morphing back into that of the stalwart Commander of the Sun Wolves. Inexhaustible. Unrelenting. A true warrior in every sense of the word. She looked down at Elya one last time.

"Think on that. Think on the decision before you. And, if we make it through this day… then, you can decide."

With that, the Paladin turned and left. Elya stared after her into the emptiness of her tent. In all of her life, silence had never been so deafening.

CHAPTER SEVEN

Over the following hours, Elya could feel her strength returning to her.

Conversation outside had slowly subsided, until eventually the camp had gone totally silent. She knew why. The Aarn were close, terribly close. Close enough that every single member of the Sun Wolves was likely already in position, waiting for the battle to come. Yet here she was, lying down and being totally useless.

She knew that she was being too hard on herself. After all, she was only knocked off her feet like this because she had used too much holy power at once to heal Dorian. She could not bring herself to think of that as a mistake, even if it now kept down.

Luce and Dorian had come back for a time after Elaine had gone, but with everything Elya had been left to think over she was unable to focus much on her friends. Eventually, they took the hint that she had a lot on her mind. Luce had gone to report in with Asani, he had said, to confirm his duties for the defense. Dorian had posted himself outside of her tent, though from the light snoring she could make out he had ended up falling asleep in the grass.

Elya cursed herself a fool for overextending, was glad to have saved Dorian from death, then cursed herself again. It was a cycle that eventually had her grinding her teeth in frustration.

At the very least, she needed to be outside. She needed to see the fight, rather than lie there awaiting whatever fate had in store for her. Maven had told them that the Horde was around ten hours out when they had met in the evening, and now it was deep into the night. She was unsure how long she had been unconscious, had not thought to ask when the others were here, and now was loathe to wake Dorian to ask.

Eventually, she had enough strength back in her body to push off the ground and sit again. Her head still hurt, but it was leagues better than it had been. Deciding to test herself, she stuck her fists to the ground and pushed, rising first to one knee, then the other. Her body shook from the exertion, but she took long breaks between each movement, allowing herself to catch her breath and wait out the weakness.

After what felt like an eternity but was likely only a few minutes' time, Elya was on her feet and stumbling as quietly as she could out from the tent. The chill of the night made her shiver, but the breeze did wonders for her mental state. It reinvigorated her as it blew, giving her the fortitude to take stock of things.

Right now, she was still fully clothed even down to the boots, likely left so on purpose by Elaine to keep her warm while her body recovered. Her swords, both practice and true, were back inside the tent. She would get them and her belt and sheathe momentarily, but first she wanted to find out what was going on.

The tent she had emerged from was set up near the gates of the abbey, so that from her position standing outside of it their defenses were laid out in full before her. She might have been frustrated that they had not allowed her into the infirmary, but was hardly surprised by it, her mind instead focused on what she saw.

Sturdy, spiked ramparts of earth and stone rose perhaps six feet from the ground in a wide semicircle before the abbey, with three large gaps spaced apart. Wolves in full battle array stood in position behind overturned supply wagons, ready to meet their foes as they entered those gaps.

What archers they had stood atop raised platforms scattered across the defenses. Glancing down at the slumbering form of Dorian, she realized that it would probably be a good idea to wake him sooner than later so that he could go and join them.

For now, she let him be.

A few scattered tents were arranged at the core of the space between the raised ramparts and the stone walls of the abbey itself, where a select few warriors stood, eyes roaming their preparations as though watching for something specific. Morgan, Elaine, Garth and Maven were among that number, along with other, older Sun Wolves she did not know by name, though she recognized some of their faces as belonging to those that had been present earlier before the visper arrived.

Asani was there, too. She was too far away from Elya to be able to tell her physical state, but the fact that she was standing on her own, armed and armored and ready to fight, was something on its own. Luce was not in that core group, but he was a fairly new member of the company and it seemed only the more experienced members stood with the Commanders. He was probably down at one of the gaps preparing to meet the Horde.

While the ramparts did not extend around the sides of the abbey, Elya knew that the only entrance into the structure were the front gates. If the Aarn truly would pass so long as those before them proved too much trouble to remove, and they were not angered by the sight of unarmed innocents, all they had to defend *was* the gate.

All in all, she was impressed. While it seemed like Maven had likely done a good portion of the heavy lifting when it came to building their fortifications, she knew every single member of the Wolves had participated in some way. They all stood together, ready to face whatever challenge came their way.

"Commander Rohadi took the visper down handily, in the end," Dorian said quietly behind her. Elya turned, looking up into the ranger's face where he had come to stand behind her. The humor she had known from him so far was gone, replaced by a tension and worry that scarred a man not meant to convey those emotions so harshly.

'Death is a constant companion to us, Elya,' Elaine had told her. *'We know it intimately, and it knows us.'*

Searching her friend's face, his constant smile dashed against random violence, she saw the truth of those words given form.

"I saw it. Right before... right before I was out," Elya replied, smiling at Dorian, who responded with a ghost of his usual grin before moving to stand beside her.

"You saved my life, El. I was dead. I had accepted it. I knew that the poison was spreading too quickly. I had seen the limits of Commander Lustra's healing and I knew that something so strong and rapid acting was beyond what she could mend by the time she would be able to get to me. But... Pantheon, *you saved me.* I owe you everything," he whispered, and her heart broke for the pain on his face. Something had shattered in him.

"It wasn't me. Not really. It was Ballian. I was just his vessel, passing on his power," she told him, but Dorian was shaking his head before she even finished.

"You don't get to diminish what you did. You were the one who channeled that power, and you could have done anything with it in that moment. There were so many 'right moves' you could have made, but you chose to save me. *You* chose that. I owe you," he fired back. Elya was shocked by the firmness of his words, the resolve in his eyes. Ballian bless him, he was serious. She smiled.

"You realize that without you I would probably be dying today, alone in the forest against the Horde. If anything, I owed you. Now we're even," she said. He grew quiet, considering.

"Fine… I can accept that, at least. If nothing else, it leaves us in perfect standing moving forward, right? I was excited to have you join before, but now I can't think of anyone else I would rather have at my back. You… you're something special, El."

Elya blushed at the compliment, turning away so that he would not see her face.

"I'm happy to call you friend, Dorian. But… I don't think I'll be joining the Fangs," she replied, turning her eyes to the moons above, their interwoven light in the clear sky such a beautiful thing. Dorian turned, eyes widening.

"What? Why?! After everything, after the Captain offered-"

"I don't think I'm cut out for all of this," Elya cut in, turning to meet the ranger's eyes once she had trained her face to normalcy again.

"Of course you are, El. You fit in so well with everyone – Abyss, you saved my life when I thought it was over! No one else could have done that. No one. How could you think you aren't capable of something you've already proven yourself in?" Dorian demanded, fists clenched at his side once more. His words made sense. She felt them in her core, in a way that triggered the heat of Ballian's touch. It helped seep the rest of her lethargy from her body, restoring her to something closer to normal. Although her body still ached, her mind rapidly recovered to its regular state, the fog that had already thinned lifting completely.

"Morgan doesn't seem to agree with you," she whispered back, and that managed to quiet him for a second before anger filled his eyes.

"What?!" he cried, turning a glare in the direction of his Commander. "What in all the levels of the Abyss did he say to you?!" he hissed. Elya, taken aback by his rage on her behalf, placed a calming hand on his shoulder.

"Dorian, calm down," she said, trying to decide how best to say this. "He wasn't the only one. Even Elaine warned me, told me about what I have to be able to take if I join you and... I don't think I can do it. I really don't."

Dorian's face turned red as he fumed, clenching his teeth and turning away to pace back and forth.

"What are they thinking?! I've never known a single person better fit to join us! Why would they throw that away?! It doesn't make any sense. It doesn't!" The Ranger was well and truly working himself into a fit by this point, and Elya grew concerned. She did not understand why this was affecting him so much, why he *cared*. They barely knew each other!

"Dory," she began, walking over to place a hand on his arm this time, making him stand still and look at her as she used his nickname. "It'll be okay. I appreciate it, what you – what all of you – have done for me. It means a lot that you care so much, even though we've barely met. But in the end, you'll all be able to move on just fine. It won't matter-"

Dorian turned, grabbing her by the arms, looking into her eyes.

"Don't you say that," he whispered. Then he leaned in. Elya startled as she realized what he intended. Her mind raced, heart beating like a hammer on an anvil, looking up at him as he drew closer... and then her hand came up, finding his chest and pushing him back. She shook her head, face flaming.

"I'm... I'm flattered... I really, truly am... but no. Not like this, not now. Maybe... Blood of the Pantheon, I won't do this. Not when I might be leaving. Not before you really know me," she told him. Dorian was frozen, face unreadable as he was rebuffed. Then, slowly, he pulled away, head lowering until he was looking down at the ground.

"I understand," he said stiffly. "I'm sorry. I should have known better. I-"

In the distance, horns sounded, roaring through the night sky. They spun, looking out past the ramparts. Out, as clouds gathered unnaturally fast in the sky, while the temperature began to drop so quickly that they were shivering in seconds.

"Pantheon help us," she gasped, watching as a roiling mass shook the trees for miles across the horizon. "Pantheon help us all."

The Horde was upon them.

"Hold, Wolves! Show no fear!" Garth roared, his lungs powering his words to travel to everyone over the distant rumble of the Aarn approach. Elya stood between Asani and Dorian among the Sun Wolf veterans, much to the aggravation of everyone. They all wanted her to stay back by the gates, where she could escape inside if the danger became too great.

She had refused, of course. At least for now. She would probably move back once the battle was truly joined, but until then she wanted to be as close as possible. The need to know what was going on was overriding her instincts for self-preservation.

"Fool girl," Morgan growled, for the umpteenth time. Elya ignored him, tired of his constant belief that he knew better than her about what she should be doing. Dorian stayed close to her side, alternating between glaring at the Commanders, shooting worried looks toward Captain Sagi, and glancing at Elya when he thought she was not paying attention. They had not been able to talk about what had almost happened, the blur of activity in the last hour taking up all her focus. But they would need to. After.

So long as there was an after.

"Until now, it was all just words..." she whispered, so quietly she did not think anyone could hear. Maven, however, cocked his head to the side and looked her way.

"Often words fail before calamity," the Wizard said, running a hand through his hair as his right foot tapped a cadence against the boot of his left. It was as though he were keeping a silent beat to some sound only he could hear.

Elya nodded to him but Maven ignored it, apparently uninterested in saying anything except the one sentence.

"Elya." Turning, she looked at Asani, whose expression was grim, her lips pursed in a thin line.

"Yes?" she asked. Glancing at the others around them, Asani sighed before continuing.

"This will be brutal. I know that our confidence paints a certain picture – and we are confident in our victory – but you have never seen bloodshed on this scale. The Aarn are in a frenzy," the Captain began, her grip tightening on the hilt of her curved blade, which Elya had learned was called a katana, while she spoke. "Their cousins to the North, the Aath, have uncovered a relic of their ancestors and prepare to face the might of the frozen tribes when they've carved their bloody path across Eran. This has happened before, which is why most nations know what to expect and plan accordingly, but we're relying a lot on their hyperfocus to make it out alive. There is no need for you to even remain outside of the abbey and see what is about to happen."

Once again, someone thought that they knew what was best for her. She closed her eyes and breathed deep, taking a moment to make sure she was in control of her emotions. She knew it was different with Asani. The Captain had not lied to her or thought less of her at any point since they met. She was genuinely concerned for her well-being. Elya would not let her frustrations with others change how she treated someone who had only proven herself a friend.

"Thank you, Asani. I appreciate you and all you've done for me, and I cannot thank you enough for making me the offer that you did, in spite of what... others may have decided about it." Elya paused, turning and not trying to hide her glare at Morgan in the slightest. Then she turned back to the captain. "All of that said, at this point I will determine what is best for me. No one else. I know that you may not understand, but I hope that you can at least respect it."

Asani looked at her for a long time, her eyes shifting back and forth as though she was looking for something. Then she closed her eyes and nodded.

"Of course I can respect that. By Orome, I even understand it," she replied, invoking a name Elya did not know. "I just wouldn't have been able to focus without at least trying."

The Captain gave her a somber smile, then looked back at all of the waiting Sun Wolves. Elya followed her gaze, taking it in. Who knew how many of them would live to see tomorrow? Already she had wounded and even maimed friends being cared for, over half of the Fangs out of commission before the battle with the Aarn had even arrived alongside what was now the lone survivor from the squad that had been attacked initially.

Even through that, however, she felt the warmth of Ballian filling her, her fears and worries like kindling to the hearth. She had faith that they would make it through. Even if what they faced was a true disaster.

They were close now. Their advance had been visible from leagues away, their skaerig -which Elya had heard mentioned before - literally changing the weather along their path. The clouds that had formed in the distance now released a dense snowstorm that looked like a wall of white in the sky. As it moved ever closer, the forest beneath became buried in ice and snow.

Maven had remarked just how much Mana was being poured into that spell, for it to cover such a large swath of land for such a long period of time.

"It's unlikely that their witches will be able to participate directly in battle, though not impossible. I should be able to nullify their spell in our area until they pass because of that. But beware – nothing is certain," Maven had said a short while ago. Elya really did not know what a skaerig witch was capable of, in comparison to a Wizard, though she knew there were many ways to command the Mana of the Nine Worlds. Different cultures developed those ways over thousands of years, which was about all she had been able to learn on the subject in Talwich Abbey's sparse library.

The different forms of spellcasting were only one of the many areas of study she intended to delve into should she make it through in one piece.

"Come on," she whispered, watching the storm grow closer. "Come on…"

Elya was shivering when the first Aarn came into view, the temperature lower than frigid. Maven had opted not to counteract the weather magic until the snowstorm itself was within reach, not just the cold it was unleashing into the environment.

Her first look at one of the creatures was still from a distance, but what she noted immediately was its size. She knew what a human looked like beside those trees. Maybe not in specific units of measurement, but relatively. The Aarn warrior she saw barreling toward their position reached the lowest branches of the trees, and her breath caught as she realized their size.

"Ballian's crown, they're huge!" she remarked, drawing a chuckle from Garth who stood beside her. He was fully armored now, though to her surprise more lightly than what Morgan or Elaine wore. He was in dense leathers with steel plates covering his joints, and he gripped an axe two-thirds his height in length with both hands. Its wicked, double-sided head was a true picture of lethal beauty. What looked like the side profile of a screaming not-quite-human figure was etched into the metal, so that it looked like the two sides of a face when viewing from either side of the weapon.

"Don't worry none, El. They bleed the same as any of us," the Half-Giant said, winking at her. By this point he was the only one who still seemed at ease.

"Garth?" Morgan said, turning back to look at him, and the oldest member of the Sun Wolves nodded back. Placing the head of his battle-axe on the ground and leaning its weight against himself, he cupped his hands around his mouth and shouted.

"SHOW THEM OUR STRENGTH!"

The Sun Wolves let out a roar as Maven shut his eyes and began to chant, his tattoos starting to glow a deep blue as he floated off of the ground. His hands and fingers twisted into arcane shapes as he spoke in a language beyond mortal ken. Mana poured out of him in slow rivers, forming intricate shapes in the air that then began to shoot into the sky. A dome of shimmering blue began to form around Talwich Abbey and the meadow it stood in, and as the snowstorm came up against it, it was turned aside.

The storm groaned and screamed like it was alive, trying to tear down the Wizard's protection, but it could not. Maven's unintelligible words began to turn into a melody that the energy of the world sang back to.

Maven hovered ten feet off the ground and continued to rise, Mana circling him still and growing faster in its movements. His eyes were lanterns of blue light so deep it reminded her of the night sky. If Elya did not have personal history interacting with the real thing and saw this, she would have said the Wizard looked like nothing less than a god made flesh.

"Eyes front El!" Dorian shouted over the cataclysmic combination of storm, Aarn battle cries in the thousands and the roaring hum of magic. "The fight is before us!"

The ranger had his bow drawn and an arrow nocked. She almost balked, the sight of so ordinary a weapon before so unordinary a threat seeming useless. Yet when she saw the others around them with their own weapons bare, when she once more took in the advancing Aarn that now poured out of the trees in an endless tide of white fur and snarling faces, she remembered that the battle led under the shelter of magical giants was what would determine victory.

The monstrous barbarians were close enough now that she could make out details. Asani had mentioned in passing that they looked like a bear crossed with something called an ape, and she could definitely see the bear, though their fur was a stark white that made them blend into the falling snow outside Maven's barrier. She only saw them in detail as they passed through that dome of Mana and into the meadow.

They were not only tall but thick, with fatty midriffs and chests and shoulders so bound in dense muscle that it was obvious even through their dense coats. That muscle continued into arms as thick around as their thighs and ending in hands the size of their massive heads. As they charged, they alternated between running on their tree trunk legs and using their fists down on all fours to boost their momentum. They wore the lightest of armor over only their most vulnerable points, their natural protections much greater than those of most sentient peoples Elya had ever heard of. Their weapons were similarly simple and looked built to make use of their immense physical strength. Spears, huge clubs or spiked knucklers on their fists were almost all that she could make out.

Elya could not even tell which were male and which were female.

"Pantheon give us strength. Syranna's light fill us. May our enemies be laid low and shatter themselves upon us," Elaine began to pray, hammer in one hand and brilliant silver shield in the other. Both began to glow with the golden light of her goddess and she raised the hammer overhead.

"To battle!" the Paladin cried.

"To battle!" Morgan howled in echo, calling his midnight black sword forth as his eyes flared to a bright yellow, pupils turning to slits. The green runes flared to life along the length of his blade.

"TO BATTLE!" Garth the Half-Giant roared, his shout ripping through the cacophony to reach the rest of the Wolves preparing to greet the Aarn with sword and axe and hammer and arrow.

"DEATH AND GLORY!" the troops roared back. They stood ready behind rampart and wagon and every defensive measure they had possessed the time to take.

Shields rose. Archers tensed. The Sun Wolves braced.

The Horde's frontline closed the distance.

Elya sucked in a breath.

A single moment passed where time stood still, the flickering of human souls burning bright against seemingly insurmountable odds.

The twang of fletching loosed as a dim, quiet opening and the first cry of pain as their battle began.

CHAPTER EIGHT

Nothing could have prepared her for the violence that erupted.

Elya thought that she had seen horror when she witnessed what the visper had visited upon her friends, and that had certainly been terrible, just as seeing its life taken by Morgan following that brief but frantic struggle had been terrible.

Yet she found immediately that there was no terror like war, and though this conflict was not as drawn out as a true war it was as bloody as any great battle between kingdoms. Worse, even, because the Horde just kept coming, heedless of the corpses of their own kind slowly piling up in front of them.

"Archers, keep your fire steady!" Garth called.

Even his booming voice could barely be heard above the onslaught, but it still did the job for now. The Wolves were making a mess of the waves of Aarn warriors that tried to storm their positions, forced to proceed through the openings in the ramparts with no way to break down walls of packed earth and rock such as those that Maven had conjured. It made for a killing field.

They only had maybe twenty or so archers among all the squads of the company, including Dorian who remained by her side. By this point she could only assume that he must be the Fang who would stay by her side, since one had to be with her at all times. That did not bother her, at least. Even if it had, seeing the carnage unfolding now would have quickly changed that.

Those archers actively engaging in the fight were able to enjoy narrow target zones to fire into, and with so few of them they could focus on accuracy rather than speed. With enemies as bulky as the Aarn, that was needed. Elya saw several take an arrow to the chest or stomach or pretty much anywhere other than their heads and completely ignore it.

These were the Sun Wolves, however, and every single person who called themselves a Wolf was one of the best at what they did. Arrows consistently found their targets in their faces or necks, dealing real damage and sometimes killing them outright. There were only three openings in the ramparts, so even when the arrows failed to kill an enemy, the circle of warriors protecting the gaps made quick work of those who squeezed through.

Right now, things seemed to be going perfectly. Even so, people took hits. It was the sheer press of them, the ferocity of apex predators unleashed in sentient form. No matter how well the Wolves performed it was inevitable that people would get hurt.

For now, none of the wounds were serious enough to remove someone from the defense.

"None of them are getting through! We're winning!" Elya shouted, and although the sight of so much blood and gore staining the green of the meadow and marring the white fur of their enemies was sickening, she was able to smile as she turned toward Dorian and Asani. When she saw their faces, though, her excitement at what seemed to be good news faded quickly.

"What's wrong?" she asked, getting close so they could hear her without having to be so loud. Asani gritted her teeth and spat in the grass before she answered.

"El, we've barely scratched the surface of their numbers. We're killing a lot, and the bodies will help stem the flow some, but our people can't keep up with this pace. It's going to exhaust everyone, and quickly," the Captain explained, hand clenching and unclenching on her hilt. That habit had never looked so frightening as it did then.

"But we don't have to kill them all, right? Isn't the plan to just make them believe it's too much of an effort to take us out?" Elya replied, looking toward the battle unfolding all around her. The slight slope of the meadow was the only reason she could see everything so clearly from the middle of the defensive positions. She was grateful for it.

Captain Sagi answered her again.

"That's the plan, yes. But with Maven preoccupied holding back the magic of their witches, it's completely up to our fighters to buy us enough time for the Horde to pass. The ones fighting us won't be willing to get left behind and should follow. It's just a matter of how long it takes for us to get there."

Grimacing, she nodded her understanding, wishing that she possessed enough strength to empower all of the men and women who were fighting. She might be able to help reinvigorate a few, but she had learned her lesson about overextending.

"Dorian!" Morgan suddenly snapped, startling the ranger. Shooting Elya and Asani a quick glance, he turned and headed over to the Commander. There were some tense words that none of them could hear, then Morgan grabbed Dorian by the front of his leather armor and practically lifted him off the ground before pushing him away. He stumbled back in their direction while the Dread Wolf refocused on the conflict.

They were all waiting to see where they would be needed most, she had realized, and it had done nothing for anyone's mood. Now that the fight had begun, even Garth's seemingly inexhaustible good mood had faded. Everyone was worried. Elya could not fault them. Yet to see her friend thrown about like that did nothing for her already low opinion of the most legendary member of the company.

"Commander Rohadi wanted me to tell you that he is no longer asking, he is ordering you to fall back behind the walls," Dorian explained with gritted teeth once he was back with Elya and Asani.

"Does he just not understand when to give something up?!" Elya replied. Pantheon preserve her, she understood less and less what Elaine saw in the man.

"Don't worry. I told him where he could shove his orders," the ranger replied, flashing an angry, worried but still very genuine smile that was much closer to the version of him she had known up until saving his life.

Elya grinned back at him, while Asani's eyes widened in alarm.

"You did what?" the Captain snapped, but she did not have time for an answer. Maven shouted from above, drawing everyone's attention.

"Reinforcements needed at the gaps! There's another surge incoming and our fighters are flagging already!" The company veterans leapt into action. Garth hefted his axe and turned, pointing to four others including Asani.

"With me, now!" he told them, and they obeyed. Captain Sagi gave Elya and Dorian a grim smile before heading off, racing toward the opening in the dead center of the ramparts, directly facing the far end of the field of battle. Those that remained, another six, split into two groups and moved up by the Commanders. Morgan and Elaine shared a few private words and then a kiss that left Elya blushing before splitting off to reinforce the other positions.

While she had not seen Garth in action, she knew that Morgan and Elaine both were forces unto themselves. She could only assume that the Half-Giant was just as strong, and that their small group of reinforcements would be able to hold as the Aarn assault continued.

Soon enough only Elya and Dorian were left standing there, watching the bloodshed continue. Elya was once again amazed as she saw the leaders of the Sun Wolves join the fight, each of them completely shifting the momentum.

Elaine's hammer burst with light with every strike, even as she called on Syranna to bolster those around her and soothe their pains. There were too many people to keep that up for long, but doing it once was simple for her. Every person who was touched by her Evocation began to glow with a soft light, and the Aarn were turned back.

Garth was a whirlwind of blood and gristle and bone, turning with great swings that carved through the Horde like so much chaff. The Half-Giant was truly a force unto himself, like a mountain around which the Aarn had to split or be smashed against him. Around him, the other warriors that had arrived at his side made quick work of any that made it through. Elya could just make out Asani darting back and forth, her blade a blur as she carved through the press.

Then there was Morgan.

If Elaine was a stalwart champion who girded those around her with the strength to keep fighting, and if Garth was a monster of a man whose sheer aggression halted the enemy advance and allowed his companions to cut down what remained, then Morgan was a one-man army.

The Wolves who had accompanied him just stood back, pulling the exhausted fighters aside while their leader, the Dread Wolf of Rohadon, unleashed a slaughter.

Nothing that came against him survived, the glowing runes of his blade leaving streaks in the air that seemed to hover a moment before dissipating. His weapon carved through flesh and innards without slowing at all, and Elya watched as the Aarn were quite literally cut into pieces. Every movement and swing of his blade made him more and more of a beast than a man in her eyes.

She could not bring herself to look away from that stand. From Morgan Arn Rohadi, as he stood against the Horde on his own and *held*.

"You can say whatever you want about his personality," Dorian remarked as he, too, stared, gripping the riser of his bow so tightly that it creaked. "But there is not a person alive who can fight the way he can."

Elya could only agree.

She may have stood there the entire battle, just watching myth in action, if not for a strange sound that carried to her.

Cocking her head to the side, she tried to pick it out again. Something about it was... different from the other noises around her, of people shouting and crying out in battle, of magic and storm roaring. She listened intently, waiting to see if it would come again.

Then she heard it, barely, drowned out by all the other noise.

A bloodcurdling scream.

Slowly, eyes widening, Elya turned to look back at the abbey as the scream cut off. The gates were still shut. No Aarn had gotten through their defenses, and certainly none had climbed the oil slick walls. Those inside should have been safe.

Another scream came and her mind turned to those inside, the women she had grown up with and her new friends, most of the Fangs, recovering from their horrible wounds. Dorian had heard it too, turning to meet her gaze with a terror on his face to match her own. He shook his head.

"El, we can't-"

But she was already running.

Elya paused only long enough to get her sword from her recovery tent near the abbey's walls before putting all her weight against one of the doors of the gate, heaving with all her strength to get it open. The smaller door could only be opened from within, forcing her to do it this way. The moment it was open enough for her to slip through she did, panting, horrible thoughts of what awaited racing through her mind.

Could they have gotten inside? How would that even be possible? They had taken precautions against anyone climbing the walls, and no one had been on the wall-walk. Everyone had taken the warnings not to be seen seriously.

More screams, multiple people now, rent the air.

Heart pounding in her chest, she lifted a prayer.

'Ballian! Syranna! Pantheon, please! Help me!'

"Elya!" a shout came from behind her as she reached the far end of the garden that the gates opened into, that open sky allowing bleak, pale light in through the storm that blotted out the sun. She noted the trampled flowers, as though something huge had landed amongst them and dragged through them all, heading deeper into the building.

"Elya, wait!" Dorian shouted again. Glancing back, she saw that he had followed her, was hot on her heels and catching up. Her mind whirled. Was he trying to stop her? Was he just going to come with her? She could not afford to stop and find out.

The Holy Core in her chest pulsed with a searing heat, so warm it almost felt like burning from the inside out. It flooded her body as Ballian's concern grew in-tune with her own. It gave her strength beyond her mortal body, letting her pull ahead of the ranger as light began to emit from her skin in a blurry aura. It reminded her of the air above a fire.

"El!" Dorian cried again, but he could no longer keep up as she peeled through the central hall that led from the garden, turning a corner and working her way through familiar places. More screams, accompanied by a deep, shuddering, sibilant hiss. A noise that was all too familiar to her. A noise she knew came from a creature that Morgan had slain, whose corpse still sat in the woods outside the abbey.

A visper.

"Elya! We can't fight it by ourselves!" her friend called down the halls, his voice echoing against the stones and reaching her still even though she could no longer see him behind her.

She knew that. Obviously, she knew that. It had taken so many to defeat the other beast, Morgan dealing the finishing blow himself. She was not his match in strength, or even any of the others. But all of this, everything she had done and faced within herself to find help for those women and for the place she had called home for her entire life, would be for naught if they died anyways.

Elya heard something crunch, more screams echoing the noise. She turned one last corner and ahead of her, she saw the back end of the beast extending into the hall outside of the chapel. The chapel, where everyone had gathered to pray for the conflict outside and so that they were all accounted for if the Aarn somehow got inside.

Now, instead of a safe place, the room had become a dining hall for an Abyssal monster.

The only consolation that she had was that it was smaller than the one Morgan had slain in the forest.

She did not think. She could not afford to. Elya gripped her hand-and-a-half blade in fists so tight the skin over her knuckles was going white with tension. She thought of the one true Evocation she had learned, the only other purposeful expression of Ballian's power she had succeeded in besides healing.

Blessed Weapon, Elaine had called it.

Elya poured all of the power she had available in her Holy Core into her sword and it erupted in flickering orange light, like the steel was made of flame. She felt her god with her. Her fear fell away, replaced with a determination to save everyone that she could. She reached the tip of the visper's tail, rounded its far side, came to the wide doors that led to the chapel and brought her weapon down with a shout.

The blade melted through the monster's armored scales, burnt through flesh and blood and cartilaginous bone before carving out the bottom and biting into the stone floor with a hiss.

Its reaction was immediate. It hissed in agony, whipping the rest of its length into the chapel even as it spun about, eyes locking on Elya as she shoved the portion of its body she had cut off aside and slipped into the room. What she saw inside chilled her.

A dozen bodies were strewn about the room, ripped apart with a wild viciousness only a being of the Abyss could be responsible for. She tried not to look at faces. She would know them all, women she had grown up with now slain as a demon's playthings. She did not have a chance to see who was still alive, cowering at the far end of the chapel behind the altar, before the visper began to move.

It spread its feathered wings as far as it could, its disturbingly human arms slamming aside pews with open hands as it released a threatening, pulsing hiss from its throat. As Elya took in its full form, she realized that the portion she had sliced away only accounted for maybe a sixth of its length, and that portion alone had been larger than her.

Her eyes met the visper's. Then it pounced.

Elya had no experience fighting monsters. She had barely practiced with her weapon against Asani, and the lack of time since then had kept them from sparring again. The beast whipped its head forward, shoving against the ground with its hands the size of her upper body and flapping its wings just once, backwards, to move even faster.

Its nasty, razor sharp fangs snapped shut barely an inch from her head.

The monster overbalanced, falling to the side as it tried to get a handle on its new length. While the portion she had managed to cut off had far from killed the thing, it was immediately obvious that its balance was off without its tail. The arms and hands helped correct that, somewhat, but it would not be perfect. Something told her that taking advantage of that very fact would be the only way she made it out of here alive.

Stepping in toward the visper's head as it pushed off the ground, Elya swung her weapon again with another cry, carving a black, burning line across the side of its face. Though she did not reach the brain, she watched as inside that wound flames flickered to life. As they burned through their minimal fuel, the visper's right eye changed to a black, crispy horror.

It reeled back with a terrible rasping sound, slamming into the chapel wall, the ceiling, shattering a wide portion of stone and mural with its weight. Too distracted by the movements of its head and arms, she did not notice the back half of its remaining length ripping through the air until it took her full in the side of her body.

She screamed as something *crunched* in her left arm, her ribs. She soared through the air and collided with the frame of the chapel's entrance, something popping threateningly in her spine as the air was blasted from her lungs. She knew without looking that the state of her arm was awful, but the white of her shattered bone stabbing through bleeding skin made her quail.

Still, she did not stay down. Could not.

Moving shakily to her feet, Elya reached for Ballian's power but felt only a trickle, a reminder that her channeled Evocation – the only reason that she could deal any damage to this monstrous foe at all – was using almost all her energy. Even that would not last much longer. Her body, barely recovered from the last time she had overtaxed it, was screaming at her to stop and rest.

The visper finally recovered, looking around wildly through its one remaining eye until it laid both, one whole and one ruined, on her struggling form. Hissing once more, it shot across the room toward her. Elya leaned against the wall, bracing herself and bringing her other hand up in front of her, still holding her sword.

She screamed, a guttural thing of pain and anger, as death came toward her.

Then an arrow whistled past her head, shooting into the roof of the visper's nostril opposite its nasty, blind eye. The shocking pain of it made the beast jerk to the side at the last second and then Elya was pulled back, through the doors, as Dorian shoved her down behind the portion of the creature's body she had burned through in the hall.

"STAY DOWN!" he shouted.

Then the full force of the visper's leap carried it through the thinner front wall of the chapel's entryway, smashing straight into her friend. He was flung through the air so quickly that barely a moment passed between going airborne and the visceral, horrible sound his body made as it flew down the hall, skipped against the ground and then slammed into another wall.

Her vision blurred. She wanted to scream again but found the sound would not come. Dorian was a bloody smear, his... Pantheon, no... his body...

Something in her snapped.

It took her a long moment to get back to her feet from where her dead friend had thrown her to save her life. The visper was so wounded, blood leaking from its nose, shaking its head vigorously from side to side to dislodge the arrow. It failed, and so turned its hateful, angry eyes on Elya.

She reached for the power in her sword and felt it shift, felt it change at her urging. Ballian's power began to condense along one edge of the blade, turning from that burning orange to a white-hot, scalding yellow. Once again the visper shot for her, jaws wide, fangs glistening with venom.

It did not reach her before she swung her weapon, and when it came in contact with the sword its entire head was burnt in twain. Dead, in an instant. The power left her, her body going limp from overtaxing her Holy Core twice in barely any time at all.

When the full weight of the serpent's corpse slammed into her, everything went black.

CHAPTER NINE

Elya floated in darkness, a vast nothingness where she alone existed.

Time was meaningless as that nothingness wrapped her up like a blanket, lulling her deeper into its depths with the promise of peace, of rest. The idea of that was so wonderful that she could not bring herself to resist. It felt like she fell for an eternity.

Perhaps she would have stayed in that place forever. She would never know, because suddenly her fall was arrested as a blazing heat erupted in her chest. It felt like she was burning from the inside out. Her mouth opened in a silent scream. She began to rise, covering the vast distance she had fallen within seconds and then continuing her ascension.

The darkness clung to her, trying to pull her back down, yet the heat within her continued to burn hotter and hotter until she glowed with it. Above her, she could finally see light, flying towards it at speeds she could have never managed alone.

She reached out a hand to the light, desperate as the heat and the glow began to fill her with a single desire: escape.

The light was so close, a great, flat expanse that filled the sky.

She approached it, silently shouting in defiance. The darkness bubbled and the sound of her own cry began to reach her. Her hand reached the light. It shattered before her, and she flew out of the darkness. Out of the depths. Into some great, blinding other place.

A voice, deep and rumbling and just as warm as the heat inside of her body, spoke to her.

WAKE UP, MY DAUGHTER. YOUR TIME HAS NOT YET COME.

So she did.

Elya shot up, screaming as she wrestled with the thick blankets that had been covering her. She looked around, wild-eyed and terrified. Snippets of memory from what felt like an eternity's worth of time in some strange, dark place flashed through her brain, but it was rapidly fading as her rational mind reasserted itself.

"Elya! Elya, calm down! You're safe!" someone was shouting, and she whipped her head around to see who it was, not able to connect voice to face until she saw Morgan for herself, hands outstretched and trying as gently as possible to restrain her, so she did not hurt herself.

The Dread Wolf looked so visibly exhausted that he had black rims around his eyes.

As she began to calm down, gasping for breath as she got control of her screaming, the relief on his face was so great that she did not know what to think. Memories, real ones, began to fall back into place as her mind finally wrapped itself around the fact that she was alive.

"What happened?" she tried to ask, but her throat was so dry it came out as an unintelligible rasp.

"By all the gods, you must be thirsty. Hold on," Morgan said, immediately recognizing the issue. He stood up and walked away for a moment, giving her the chance to see where she was as she followed his movement. The familiar stonework and ceiling murals told her that she was inside Talwich Abbey, and from the cots set up throughout the room and the size of the hall she knew that this could only be the abbey's infirmary. It seemed the Daughters had finally come around to letting them use the space.

It had been seldom used growing up, but now looked mostly filled. There were some thirty cots in the room, and all but two had someone lying in them, wounded in some fashion or another. Soreness racked her body now that she had calmed down, but as she remembered the blow that had knocked her out she was confused as to where the worst of her wounds had gone.

Only dull aching remained where she knew shattered bone and torn flesh had once been.

Elya had the wherewithal to cringe at the screaming she had unleashed. Several people were sitting up or trying to and looking her way. She waved her hand awkwardly, hoping that the movement could convey her apology. Whether it did or not, those who had stirred mostly went back to sleep or at least turned over to face away.

"Is everything alright, Lord?" someone whispered. She turned her attention back to Morgan, who was being addressed by a young lady in a tan habit that marked her as one of the Daughters. With a jolt, she realized that it was Penna. One of her oldest friends was here, and yet she spoke to Morgan instead of coming to Elya's side?

"It's fine. Sleep terrors, I think, though I'm almost glad of them since she's finally awake," Morgan quietly replied. Penna nodded, gave a quick glance toward Elya, then turned and hurried away when their eyes met. Was that… was she afraid of her?

"Pehmmm," she tried to call out, but her throat was still too dry for anything but a loud croak. It was a miracle she had been screaming when she woke up. Her former friend scurried from the room. She tried to pretend, for her own sake, that it did not hurt.

Morgan returned to her side after filling a small glass with water from a pitcher on a cart that sat against the wall. Elya was settled near the back of the infirmary, with the two empty bunks separating her and the others. Being there felt surreal.

"Here, drink slowly. If you do it too quickly you're going to choke," the normally taciturn man instructed, gingerly lifting the glass toward her lips until she took it for herself. Despite her desperate thirst, she did as Morgan said and took long, measured sips. She could feel her throat being soothed as she did.

Morgan returned to the seat he had been resting in next to her bed and waited silently until the glass was empty, reaching to take it from her.

"Do you need more?" he asked, but Elya shook her head. The water had helped enough for her to be able to focus on how bizarrely the Commander was acting.

"Why... are you... here...?" she asked. Then, eyes widening as she remembered the battle with the Horde, she hurriedly continued. "What... happened... with... the Aarn?!"

She hated the gasping breaths she had to take every couple of words. Morgan raised his hands placatingly, then rubbed his eyes with a groan.

"We held against the Horde for three hours before they finally decided we weren't worth the effort and lives it was costing them. Once most had passed, even Maven was able to join in since the power of their witches' magic was mostly focused in the front of their host. Which was good... because Elaine was pulled in here, when someone finally had the brains to come and get help."

The last sentence left him in a growl, his eyes flaring into that feral, shining yellow for just a moment before he caught himself and closed them.

"Dorian... ?" Elya asked, tears springing to her eyes as she saw again in her mind the moment he was dashed against the abbey's wall, the noise he had made, but she had to know. Had to hear it confirmed by someone else. From the way his expression tightened and his lips pressed into an angry line, she knew what he was going to say before he said it.

"There was nothing we could do for Little Dory. I'm so sorry."

Elya began to sob, bringing her blanket up to cover her mouth to try and stifle the noise so she did not disturb anyone. Yet she could not stop the tears, her shoulders heaving as they flowed.

It was not long before she found herself drifting off, her weeping freshly exhausting her. Morgan carefully pulled her blanket up, but she was barely able to register that before sleep took her.

It was day the next time Elya awoke, and light was streaming into the room. Bleary eyed, she stretched, her tight muscles loosening as a wave of relief passed through her body.

'*Ballian be praised,*' she thought, staring up at the ceiling. '*No dreams at all.*'

When she looked around the room, she realized that barely half the cots were filled now. Whether that was good or bad, she could not say. Nor could she devote the mental strength needed to consider the negative possibilities.

Instead, she focused on something else. The slumbering swordswoman sitting beside her, head leaned back against the wall as she snored. Seeing Asani like that made a horribly childish giggle emerge unbidden. The noise startled the other woman awake and she leaned forward in her seat with a jerk. Elya grinned.

"You look as tired as I feel," she rasped. Her throat was parched again, but it was nowhere near as awful as it had been when she awoke in the night with Morgan.

The Captain breathed a great sigh and smiled ruefully.

"It's been a lot," Asani replied, before clasping her hands together. The smile was already gone and with it the breath of levity they had shared. Here was someone Elya could ask her most dreaded questions. Here was someone who likely dreaded the answers more than her.

"How long?" she started. Asani looked down.

"A week. The Horde passed a week ago. Elaine was worried that you…"

She trailed off.

"How many?" Elya asked, barely able to make herself say the words.

Asani scowled.

"We lost twenty-two people. Twenty-two friends and comrades, gone. Eight of the Daughters to the second visper. And Dorian-" she bit off her own words, choking on them.

"I know," Elya whispered back, tired of crying yet unable to stop the sting in her eyes. "Morgan told me."

For a while after that the two of them sat in silence, both mourning in their own way as those deaths settled deep inside of her. Asani ended up breaking the silence first.

"We should have known," she growled, her fists dropping to her knees as she clenched them. "Vispers like to hunt alone, but that doesn't mean they're solitary monsters. Several times when there have been sightings, it's been proven that they'll travel in family units. The one that…"

She took a steadying breath, forged on.

"The one that got in here, that... that killed Dorian, that almost killed you, was young. Probably the offspring of the first one. We should have known this was possible. We should have known!" Asani punched her left knee, hard, but managed to release a visible amount of rage in doing so.

"Don't blame yourself..." Elya said, quietly. The other woman looked up, eyes drawn tight in a frown. She opened her mouth to reply, but Elya shook her head. "If we try and look for someone to blame... for all this... the list would be more than just you... or even me. I hate what happened... but everyone here... chose to be here. No one was forced into anything."

As she spoke, she found the strength of her voice returning. It was a welcome feeling. Asani looked into her eyes, deep into them, for a long while. Then she slumped back in her chair, groaning.

"I'm an experienced fighter and a member of the Sun Wolves, for gods' sakes, but here I am needing a woman fresh off her first blooding to console me. Whether it's Orome, or your Pantheon, or some other deity, someone in the heavens has a horrible sense of humor," she grumbled. Then the two women burst into laughter that filled the infirmary. Once again eyes turned her way, but for this Elya did not care.

The pain – the loss – was still there. She knew that it would be for a long time, maybe forever. But in that moment, as they shared in that laughter, she knew that everything would be okay.

"Do you want to see anyone? If you're up for it, I can help you get around and visit. Commander Lustra will want to see you anyways, to know how you're doing," Asani said as their bout of laughter finally came to an end. Elya considered for a moment, thinking through those she had met since Dorian had found her. If she had been unconscious for the greater part of a week, then she had known these people for two. Ballian's crown, only two weeks and yet she already felt as though being separated from those who remained would be unbearable. With that thought, her mind turned to Morgan and Elaine, the secret they had been keeping. The conversation she had had with Morgan, his obvious desire that she not join the company.

"Yes," Elya said, smiling brightly at Asani. "I would love to see everyone!"

After that, she would see Elaine.

Then... then, she would have words with Morgan.

It was wonderful seeing everyone at least awake and on the mend, if not fully there yet. Fahra pulled her into a hug that Asani had to break because she refused to. The twins greeted her with tired smiles, especially Harn. Luce was all teary-eyed and sweet.

After the battle, and once the life-threatening injuries that came from it were tended to, Elaine had worked with Maven to undo the damage and rot done to his arm and reattached it with what was supposedly a very painful joining of Evocation and spellcraft. Now he had a massive, ugly scar from the bottom of his neck across to his shoulder. Meanwhile Ornn wore a patch over one eye socket where he had lost his eye. There would be no more mixing the two up. Luce just gave her a quick hug before sitting down, smiling contentedly.

Finally Riley greeted her, though it was with a simple, firm handshake.

"I'm glad you're alright," the very-tall woman rumbled, and that was that.

They all spent about an hour together, chatting happily over a simple lunch in the mess hall. All too soon, though, it was time for Elya to move on. With the Captain by her side to make sure was steady, she stood.

"El," Fahra said, while the others all stood as well, looking at each other quietly before she continued. "Screw what anyone says. The Commanders can go to the Abyss if they won't let you join us. Whatever happens, you're one of us."

Echoes of approval came Harn, Ornn, Riley, Luce and, to Elya's surprise, even Asani hummed in agreement.

"Thanks," she choked out, then chuckled as she wiped fresh tears away. "I'm so tired of crying." They laughed with her.

Asani took her by the shoulders, gently indicating it was time to get moving. She understood. She knew that by now, news that she was out and about would have spread. Elaine would be waiting to see her and then, that last, dreaded conversation...

Their walk through the abbey's vaunted halls, across the garden and then out the front gates stole Elya's breath. They paused a moment outside, Asani helping her slump to the ground to rest against the wall. Their break lasted for just a few minutes, both of them quietly content, before the Captain hefted her back to her feet and they continued.

The meadow in front of the abbey was still a mess, though noticeably better than Elya knew it would have been right after the fight. Maven must have returned the ramparts to the earth because they were gone. Where the gaps had been the grass and flowers had been torn into nasty, pitted earth. She tried to ignore the fact that the bare earth, visible from the gates, was tinged red.

In the place that Elya had once stood watching the battle with the leaders of the Sun Wolves, a few tents had been erected. Not a full camp's worth since they had an actual structure for many of their members to stay in right now, but there was a grouping of nine tents in varying greens and browns all surrounding that familiar large one.

For a moment she thought their destination *was* the command center, but Asani directed her to one of the others. Nothing about its exterior revealed it as any different from the others. They paused outside of it and Asani cleared her throat.

"Commander Lustra, I'm here with Elya," she said aloud.

Just seconds passed before the tent's entrance was yanked aside and the Paladin emerged. She had returned to her simple clothes with her tabard atop them, but the sheer exhaustion she exuded dulled her usual brilliance. Her hair looked even grayer than the last time she had seen her, done up in a bun with strands loose in her face.

"Blood of the Pantheon!" Elaine exclaimed, walking right up to Elya and pulling her into a firm hug. When she stepped back, she kept her hands on Elya's shoulders as she looked her over. "It's so good to see you awake and moving, El, you have no idea. The thought of you dying..."

Tears welled up in Elaine's eyes, surprising her. She knew that the woman liked her, but this? Combined with Morgan's odd behavior when she had awoken that first time in the middle of the night, she fought the urge to dive straight into questioning the woman.

She wanted to have that conversation with Morgan, so she had to restrain herself. Instead, she allowed Elaine to poke and prod her all over. Elaine appeared determined to perform a very thorough examination, refusing to say another word until she was done.

"Well, you're going to feel exhausted for a very long time, and the soreness will stick around a while too. But other than that, I'd say you're looking beyond wonderful considering what happened. I assume that's not just because of me?"

Elya nodded.

"I... can't remember the details. But I think Ballian spoke to me again while I was unconscious. I know I felt his power. If not for that, then I don't think I would be standing here in front of you," she answered, speaking honestly.

Elaine's lips grew taut with regret before she sighed and nodded.

"When I saw you, Syranna's light... I was shocked you had even lived the short time it took me to run there."

Elya could not think of herself in that state. Not right now, not with what she had to do after this. Instead, she smiled as honestly as she could.

"Thank you, Elaine. For saving me," she replied.

"Do you wish to talk? I know we've been keeping some things from you, and that you're angry about that, but after everything that's happened, I owe you answers. So does my husband."

Elya was surprised by the offer, but after considering it for a moment she shook her head.

"Thank you. For... being willing to do that. But there's only one person I want to hear answers from right now. After our last conversation, he owes me that much," she answered. The Paladin sighed but nodded.

"I understand," Elaine told her.

"As do I." She recognized the voice. Of course she did. The three women turned to see Morgan, once more in full armor, standing behind them.

His eyes roamed across the three women before he gave Elaine a small smile. Then he stood at attention, motioning with a tilt of his head.

"Let's speak, Elya. If you're to have the truth... then there's a lot of it to be had."

Elya stood across the tent from Morgan as she waited for him to speak. The long table that had been set in the center of this monstrosity of canvas the last time it had been put up was now pushed to the side, leaving a large open space.

Garth and Maven had been here when they first entered. Maven had given her a perfunctory nod, but Garth had wrapped her up in his arms gently and whispered that he was glad she was okay. Then the gigantic softie grabbed the Wizard by his arm and yanked him out, leaving her to face one of the most famous warriors alive on her own.

It might have been exactly what she wanted, but she did not have to like it.

The awkwardness felt like a rope around her throat, killing every word that she tried to say before it ever left her. Meanwhile, Morgan had walked to the far wall and had been standing in front of a large chest, staring at it.

After a godsawful wait, he finally spoke.

"There's a reason I warned you away from us. A reason I don't want you to join us, even though it feels right – and not just for you, but for me as well. I know who you are, El."

Morgan looked back at her and smiled sadly before turning back and kneeling on the ground, hands reaching toward the locked clasp that held the chest in front of him shut. A key she had not even noticed him holding slipped into that lock and turned with a click.

"Then why? I know we haven't known each other for long, but it's like you said. You already know me! If you feel like it's right for me to join the Sun Wolves, the way that I do, then what could possibly keep you from agreeing to it? You're the Dread Wolf, for Ballian's sake!" Elya exclaimed, the words coming out in an angry rush before she could get control of her emotions. Morgan slipped the key to the chest into a pouch on his belt, then lifted the lid.

"That title means nothing to me, Elya, except as a reminder of my failures. And you aren't listening to me. I did not say that I have come to know you. I said that *I know who you are*," he replied. Then he pulled something out of the chest and stood, turning to face her. It was an oblong object, longer than her sword... which she realized she did not know the location of.

Then her brain finished processing what Morgan had just told her and her eyes snapped up, searching his face. His expression was still. More than that, there were tears in his eyes as he slowly began to unwrap the object in his hands, wrapped as it was in old fabric.

"You... you know who I am?" Elya repeatedly dumbly. Morgan nodded gravely at her, then grasped the object beneath the fabric and pulled it forth, the pale silver-steel of it shining bright even in the dimness of the tent.

"I know who you are, Elya, because I knew your father and your mother. I know, because I brought you here as a baby, before the Sun Wolves ever rose to be what we are. I know," here Morgan broke, the tears falling down his face, "because your father was my very best friend in all this world, all the way up until the day he and your mother died."

He lifted the object by its hilt and revealed to her the most beautiful sword she had ever seen. Long, folded steel that curved back and forth into some impossible wave-like construction of the blade connected to a cross guard forged into a graceful crescent. The hilt was inlaid with a beautiful design done in shimmering silver, then wrapped in a deep black leather stitched with Runescript that glowed with silvery light. Its pommel was set with a round piece of crystal that was filled with the same glow, fine silver-steel prongs holding it in place.

Elya looked back and forth between the sword and the face of the man holding it with mouth agape, trying to understand. He spoke in Common, yet for some reason it was as though her mind could not comprehend his words.

Emotion, from some deep place she thought sealed forever when she finally grew up enough to set aside the idea of knowing where she came, exploded out of her. Her shoulders heaved. She gasped, but the air wouldn't settle in her lungs right. She closed her eyes, as though to find safety in lidded vision.

Her legs shook as she took a step toward Morgan, reaching toward him like he was a lifeline.

When he let that beautiful sword fall, grasped her hand and held her, she let go even if only for a moment. She released every bit of emotion she was feeling. Then, she pulled herself back together with sheer determination. After all, she needed to know more.

"What happened?" she managed to get out between deep breaths. Now that she could speak again, Morgan let go of her and backed away, awkwardly clearing his throat before bending over to pick the sword up. Thankfully the canvas floor of the tent had kept it from getting dirty, at least. Once he had the blade in his hands again, he answered.

"The three of us - me, Elaine and your father? It was just us when we started out. Elaine and I both had our circumstances, lives we had to leave behind due to things outside of our control. But Harald Dalgaard, well, he was used to hard living. He came from a farmstead in the Northern reaches of the continent, where the Nothkiri roam in their skyships, raiding and plundering. He was the youngest of six, so when he came of age he had no inheritance to claim and struck out alone. Circumstance led him also to join the armies of the United Jarls, fighting back against the Noth. He learned to fight in one of the longest ongoing wars in Eran's history, then came South as mercenary when his service was up. He far more experienced than us when we met."

Morgan's eyes were distant as some long ago memory played through his mind.

"Elaine can share how he found her some time, but I was the last. I fled my homeland of Rohadon, cast out by my family and left with nothing but a title that I hated – the Dread Wolf. The Midnight Sun title came later, but I was already the 'Dread' when they found me stumbling along the road between Miradar and Loras, half-dead from a bandit attack and with all but my armor taken from me. I was so delirious, starving and devastatingly thirsty, that I was sure that they were the bandits, returned to finish me off."

He paused here, closing his eyes as if he were actually trying to see those times now past. Then he shook his head, looking back at Elya.

"I won't bore you with all the details of what led to us becoming more than strangers united by chance, but the three of us wound up as family. I fell in love with Elaine, and Harald was like a brother to us both. We fought as a trio all over the Middle Kingdoms for three years before he met *her*," Morgan said, chuckling. "Before he met your mother."

Elya was entranced, unable to think or act or even speak as Morgan told his tale. She knew her father's name. Harald – Northern name for sure! She had to wonder if, somewhere up in that land of heat and strange, sparse savannah, she yet had family toiling away with no idea of her existence.

That thought was but a passing fancy, however, before the idea of learning her mother's name too. Morgan could see the eagerness in her eyes and did not delay his continuance.

"We met your mother when we rescued a small town from a band of Greenskins. She lived there, the daughter of a farmer, much the same as Harald's own humble beginnings. We could tell from the look in his eyes that your father was taken with her from the start. He used to call her 'his blessed Aelya,' from the moment they began to see each other all the way up until he passed from this world."

The pain that flashed across his face was there and gone so quick she almost did not notice it. Almost.

"It was when they decided to marry that Harald had the idea to build something. A legacy for his family, beyond blood. A banner to rally the lost and broken. He took the name from pieces of my past, of Elaine's – the sun from Elaine's bond with Syranna, the wolf to redeem what I hated most about myself. The Sun Wolves. And Harald, Aeyla... they were our moons."

Morgan grew quiet and the silence stayed for a time. Elya needed it, needed the space to process the information being given to her. She had no idea what to think and had yet to learn why, if all of this was true, she had been abandoned at the abbey.

"If so... if... if my parents were there at the founding of the Sun Wolves... then why? Why don't you want me to join you?" she finally managed to ask. Quietly. Afraid that she would not like the answer but needing it anyways.

Morgan's expression swiftly shifted to something dark, something pained.

"Because when your father died in my arms, Elaine and I promised that you would never know the horror of a life of bloodshed, El. That you would grow up surrounded by peace. Your mother was a follower of Ballian, so I thought that you should go to the church that she held so dear. Even though your experience with some of his followers has been... difficult... your bond with Ballian now seems to me proof that it was the right thing to do."

This fresh revelation was once again enough to bring silence. This time, however, it was charged – with sadness, yes, but even more so with Elya's rage.

"So..." she began, starting quietly. "My parents help form this company... my father specifically wanted it to be his legacy, for his family and the family he had created with you... so when he and my mom... when they die, your big idea is to SHIP ME OFF AND NEVER TELL ME ANYTHING?!"

Morgan startled at the force of her yell, letting the tip of the sword fall towards the ground as he adjusted his grip to one hand.

"You don't understand, El. This life, it's... it can be horrific. We wanted you to be able to have a normal life. But we knew that if you were with us, if you grew up in this, then it would become all you knew. We didn't want that. I know that your parents wouldn't have-"

"NO!" Elya snapped, interrupting the man like he was not the most dangerous person she had ever known. "You don't get to say that. You don't get to decide what you think they would have wanted. This should have been something that I decided, for myself, when I was old enough to. Instead, you took the ability to choose from me. I am grateful for my bond with Ballian, and I love my sisters dearly, but the Order? Blood of the Pantheon, I spent years acting like someone I'm not out of fear, so that I wouldn't be reprimanded, or beaten, or..."

This seemed to be a conversation for trailing off, because once more she grew quiet, not able to find the words she needed to say to this man. This idiotic, fool of a man. Elaine, too! They had both known who she was, so she was equally at fault for allowing this to happen – for agreeing to it in the first place!

She could have had an entirely different life. Eyes hardening, she decided.

"Well, you don't get to decide for me anymore. Never again. So help me Ballian, Syranna, Maldior, Thoras, Vectan... all the gods of the Pantheon! If you do not let me join the Wolves I will strike out on my own and find a different group to fight for. Maybe I'll go North and enlist in the military like my father! Maybe I'll join another mercenary group! Whatever I decide to do, Abyss take you, you have no right to say otherwise!"

This proved too much for Morgan, whose face twisted in rage. He took a step toward Elya, eyes flaring to that bright yellow as he growled.

"You stupid girl! You'll go and get yourself killed! I won't allow you to just go out and die after all this!" he snarled, his voice booming... but Elya grinned.

"Well then, if you don't want me to go out on my own and die, as you say, there's no choice but to let me join you, is there?" she interjected before the angry warrior could say another thing. Morgan's eyes widened and his mouth clamped shut immediately, whatever else he was about to yell evaporating into nothing.

"Huh?" he asked. Elya walked up to him, still smiling, and slapped him clear across the face. Then she stuck a finger up under his nose and hissed.

"And if you ever presume to tell me what you will or won't 'allow me' to do again, I will make your life a living hell. Do you understand me, uncle?"

Morgan Arn Rohadi, a living legend, stared at her dumbfounded, his free hand coming up to his cheek where the red outline of her hand was visible. He had no idea how to respond, how to turn things back around on her. Elya's face returned to a smile as she backed away.

"Now, why did you get that sword out?" she asked, looking down to that gorgeous weapon still gripped in the man's hand.

"It, um..." he started, trailed off, looked down at what he held before shaking his head and continuing. "It was your father's. I was going to... to give it to you, so that you would have something of his to remember him by."

That got her attention. Of course it did.

"What?!" she exclaimed, reaching for it immediately. Morgan, still in a state of shock, slowly brought it up, adjusting his hold on it so that he could give it to her hilt first. She hefted the weapon, holding up so that the flat of one side faced Morgan and the other faced her. After a moment, to both their surprise, the silvery light the weapon was giving off from its Runescript and blade suddenly surged and changed, morphing as Elya felt the now familiar flare of Ballian's power rising inside of her.

The heat flowed down her arms, through her hands and into the weapon. It turned what was silver to the reddish orange of embers, like fire the moment before it ignited. As the transformation was completed and the heat began to fade from her body, she noted one other change – the gem embedded in the blade's pommel had become amber, with what looked like a tiny flame burning inside.

Victory. That was what Elya felt as she once more looked up at Morgan, crooking her eye as though to ask him if he truly had anything else to say to try and convince her not to join them all when it was time to go. He said nothing. Could say nothing. So with a *humph,* she turned and started for the exit of the tent.

"I'll be ready to go whenever, Commander," she called over her shoulder. Then she was outside, leaving Morgan to stare helplessly after her.

And despite it all, despite his frustration and the fact that he still believed he was right, he smiled. Pantheon help him, he smiled. Elya had called him uncle.

Two days later, when the last of their wounded were back on their feet, the Sun Wolves left Talwich Abbey behind, following the great, trampled path of the Horde up toward the central regions of Caldria.

The Daughters of Ballian saw them off with little fanfare. Yet the smile on Elya Dalgaard's face as she laughed with Asani, and Fahra, and the rest of her new family did not falter before their stares. She strode right along with the company, her new sword across her back.

She still had a lot to learn about her family, her parents. But she had all the time in the world to do so, to speak with Morgan and Elaine.

She was a Sun Wolf, after all. Like her father before her, with her mother's faith in her heart. Nothing had ever felt more *right*.

ABOUT THE AUTHOR

Denver Binion is a writer and author of his debut novella, The Sun Wolves. Twenty-six years old and married to the love of his life, with whom he is raising his almost two-year-old son in McKinney, TX, Denver has been an avid reader with a deep love for the Fantasy and Science Fiction genres since he was a young child. When he's not writing or working, you can usually find him indulging in his deep love for books in a quiet space, exploring realms unknown with his Dungeons & Dragons group, or most often of all hanging out with his family and trying to explain the differences between a Wizard, a Mage and a Sorcerer.

Made in the USA
Columbia, SC
20 May 2024

35539099R10088